Danya...

Safe, big, strong, masculine...sensual, hot, hungry...
fierce lover, taking, giving...tender friend, sharing...

Flipside: Brooding, arrogant, traditional, a family
man if ever there was one. Worse, he cooked and
cleaned and washed her clothing and seemed content
that she had no housekeeping skills whatsoever.

The whole tall, muscular, good-looking package was
irritating, unsuitable for the lifestyle that she had
wanted.

I love you, he'd said.

Just maybe she'd been on the rebound and had
gotten blindsided by Danya.

Who was he, anyway?

But she knew. Danya was a part of her now, a man
who had shared her body, making love, not having
sex with her. Now that was scary. Lovemaking was
more than sex and now, no thanks to Danya, she
knew the difference.

It would probably haunt her forever.

Dear Reader,

Welcome to another scintillating month of passionate reads. Silhouette Desire has a fabulous lineup of books, beginning with *Society-Page Seduction* by Maureen Child, the newest title in DYNASTIES: THE ASHTONS. You'll love the surprises this dynamic family has in store for you…and each other. And welcome back *New York Times* bestselling author Joan Hohl, who returns to Desire with the long-awaited *A Man Apart,* the story of Mitch Grainger—a man we guarantee won't be alone for long!

The wonderful Dixie Browning concludes her DIVAS WHO DISH series with the highly provocative *Her Fifth Husband?* (Don't you want to know what happened to grooms one through four?) Cait London is back with another title in her HEARTBREAKERS series, with *Total Package.* The wonderful Anna DePalo gives us an alpha male to die for, in *Under the Tycoon's Protection.* And finally, we're proud to introduce author Juliet Burns as she makes her publishing debut with *High-Stakes Passion.*

Here's hoping you enjoy all that Silhouette Desire has to offer you…this month and all the months to come!

Best,

Melissa Jeglinski

Melissa Jeglinski
Senior Editor
Silhouette Desire

Please address questions and book requests to:
Silhouette Reader Service
U.S.: 3010 Walden Ave., P.O. Box 1325, Buffalo, NY 14269
Canadian: P.O. Box 609, Fort Erie, Ont. L2A 5X3

TOTAL
PACKAGE
CAIT LONDON

Published by Silhouette Books
America's Publisher of Contemporary Romance

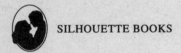 SILHOUETTE BOOKS

ISBN 0-373-76642-4

TOTAL PACKAGE

Copyright © 2005 by Lois Kleinsasser

This edition published by arrangement with Harlequin Books S.A.

® and TM are trademarks of Harlequin Books S.A., used under license.
Trademarks indicated with ® are registered in the United States Patent
and Trademark Office, the Canadian Trade Marks Office and in other
countries.

Visit Silhouette Books at www.eHarlequin.com

Printed in U.S.A.

Books by Cait London

Silhouette Desire

The Loving Season #502
Angel vs. MacLean #593
The Pendragon Virus #611
The Daddy Candidate #641
†*Midnight Rider* #726
The Cowboy #763
Maybe No, Maybe Yes #782
†*The Seduction of Jake Tallman* #811
Fusion #871
The Bride Says No #891
Mr. Easy #919
Miracles and Mistletoe #968
‡*The Cowboy and the Cradle* #1006
‡*Tallchief's Bride* #1021
‡*The Groom Candidate* #1093
‡*The Seduction of Fiona Tallchief* #1135
‡*Rafe Palladin:*
   Man of Secrets #1160

‡*The Perfect Fit* #1183
†*Blaylock's Bride* #1207
†*Rio: Man of Destiny* #1233
†*Typical Male* #1255
§*Last Dance* #1285
‡*Tallchief:*
   The Homecoming #1310
§*Slow Fever* #1334
§*Gabriel's Gift* #1357
A Loving Man #1382
‡*Tallchief: The Hunter* #1419
**Mr. Temptation* #1430
**Instinctive Male* #1502
**Hold Me Tight* #1589
**Total Package* #1642

Silhouette Books

Spring Fancy 1994
"Lightfoot and Loving"

Maternity Leave 1998
"The Nine-Month Knight"

‡*Tallchief for Keeps*

Silhouette Yours Truly

Every Girl's Guide To...
Every Groom's Guide To...

*The MacLeans
†The Tallchiefs
†The Blaylocks
§Freedom Valley
**Heartbreakers

CAIT LONDON

is an avid reader and an artist who plays with computers and maintains her Web site, www.caitlondon.com. Her books reflect her many interests, including herbs, driving cross-country and photography. A national bestselling and award-winning author of category romance and romantic suspense, Cait has also written historical romances under another pseudonym. Three is her lucky number; she has three daughters, and her life events have been in threes. Cait says, "One of the best perks about this hard work is the thrilling reader response."

One

The midnight moon hung over the Pacific Ocean's black swells like a sly curse waiting to fall. Thickening clouds slid across that silvery surface, foretelling rain.

Below the cliff on which Danya Stepanov stood, the waves caressed the smooth silvery strip of sandy beach. Alone and brooding, Danya stared at the small cluster of lights that signified Amoteh, the town in southwest Washington State.

In the distance, jutting out into the darkness was the Amoteh Resort, managed by Danya's cousin, Mikhail. The lush resort, one of a worldwide chain, offered tourists rest and businesses convention facilities. It also supplied many of the residents in town with an income from their crafts. Within the huge resort was a display room for Stepanov Furniture; the pieces were crafted by Danya's uncle Fadey, his cousin, Jarek, and others.

Winds swept up from the shoreline below the cliff, tearing at Danya's hair. Carrying the fresh bite of salt and the earthy fragrances of mid-June, the mist stirred around his body.

He turned to the ancient rocky grave, no more than a weathered mound behind him and walked to it.

The wind stirred the grass at his work boots, as if the Hawaiian chieftain who had died there recognized another lonely male. Danya understood the Hawaiian chieftain's curse upon the land, a dying man damning his fate. Kamakani had been captured by whalers over a century and a half ago, and he'd been stranded on a land that wasn't his, missing a woman who belonged to him.

Danya knew what it was to miss part of his heart and soul, his love, a wife who had died too young.

Familiar with brooding and loneliness at midnight, Danya looked around him. Strawberry Hill, a peninsula jutting out into the Pacific Ocean, was windswept and accessed by a rocky path. During high tide the waterway passage from the peninsula to the small town of Amoteh was dangerous. The huge deadly stone rising out of the crashing waves had already caused many boaters' deaths. At low tide, Strawberry Hill could be reached by a long walk along the shoreline and a hike up that rocky path.

Danya found what he wanted—a small stand of wind-whipped trees, nothing like the soaring straight pines of his native Wyoming mountains—but it held the scent and feel of home.

An experienced woodsman, Danya moved into the shadows of the trees to brood.

Nine years ago, a drunken driver had taken the life of Danya's young wife. Danya had been driving—how could he have avoided the crash, those headlights crossing the road?

Danya had lived that nightmare many times—what could he have done?

He inhaled the salty air and felt his heart twist, as if part of it had been wrenched away. His brother, Alexi, had also been a rancher, starting a new life in Amoteh. Now, over a year later, he was married and a father. Would it actually help Danya's empty heart to relocate with his father, Viktor?

Last year, Danya had desperately needed the change from

his father's Wyoming ranch, where everything reminded him of his wife. Jeannie would have liked Amoteh, a Chinook name for the wild strawberries growing in the southwest Washington State coastal area. She would have liked the tourist pier, the sailboats skimming along the horizon, and digging in the sand for razor back clams.

She would have loved raising children amid their Stepanov cousins.

He inhaled unevenly and wondered if she was there with him, swirling around in the mist, waiting….

Danya turned his thoughts to what he did have—a family surrounding him, children to hold, a growing building and remodeling business with his brother—

The sound of a stick breaking caused him to tense—someone walked through the grass. The steady sounds said that one person had purpose, tramping to a familiar destination without the use of a flashlight.

He smiled grimly; there were others walking in the night, shielding their loneliness from those who cared and worried about them.

A high loud howl broke the night—a frustrated sound too high for a man, but still a howl. Danya eased aside in the shadows, watching the small shadow cross in front of him. It tossed a bulky object to the ground in front of Kamakani's grave.

The person turned and lifted arms high—and a woman removed her top, bending to shimmy out of her loose pants.

A woman with hair too short to be caught by the wind stood, her legs braced apart, a small curvy silhouette, but definitely a woman. Outlined by the moon peeking through the clouds, she seemed almost mystical, a goddess coming to court the night.

Then she raised her hands high and yelled angrily, "Dammit, what's wrong with me? Look at me, will you, Chief? I've got everything any other woman has—maybe less in some places, but the basic equipment is there. So why did Ben marry some little fluff-cake and not me? Fluffy hasn't got a brain in her head. So why did he pick her over me?"

A string of unladylike curses sailed through the night air, and Danya had the uneasy suspicion that the lady just might intend something drastic—like stepping off that cliff onto the jagged rocks below.

"Look. Basic thirty-year-old female equipment. Correction: prime equipment. We had sex. Sure, Ben never took that long, but then we didn't have much time between jobs and that suited me. Look. Breasts. They have nipples and everything."

The woman flung away a scrap of something, that just could have been a bra. She shimmied and tugged at her hips, and her foot kicked away another scrap. "Okay, Chief. You're a man—or you were. What's wrong with me?"

Absolutely nothing was wrong with her. The woman's silhouette was all curves. Danya's throat dried and something he thought had died started stirring. She was right: all the basic equipment was there. The impact shot right down his body and lodged into a hard tight knot.

"Okay, so I don't do the helpless little Fluffy-no-brains act. That's all fake anyway. Really, Chief. Tell me. Send some sign or something."

Danya should leave her to grieve over her lost lover.

But she just might step over that cliff and that would be a shame.

Then, he thought as he weighed his options, there was the little matter of his own curiosity.

Danya moved silently through the shadows and circled down the rocky path leading to the grave site. When he'd gotten a distance down Strawberry Hill, he called loudly to the night, "I'll be fine. Go on back down without me."

Satisfied that would warn the woman of his coming, he began a slow upward walk to where he expected she would be rapidly dressing. From the corner of his eye, he noted a sleeping bag spread on the ground. His foot tangled in something and he reached down to collect a stretchy garment; it was a woman's sports bra, which he'd seen other women wearing as they worked out. The rumpled white cotton briefs were still warm and fragrant from her body. That light floral scent of a female caused him to tense, suddenly aware that it had been a long, long time since he'd made love. He crushed the fabric possessively in his fist and forced himself to toss it carelessly to the sleeping bag. "Huh. Leftovers from a romantic night I guess," he said loudly.

Danya walked slowly past the woman hidden by the night; rustling sounds said she still wasn't finished dressing, and giving her more time, he walked to the edge of the cliff.

He could hear her breathing, and sensed her waiting behind him. Then she cleared her throat. "Um, mister. You're not thinking of jumping, are you? Please don't do that. I've had a really miserable day and you'd only make it worse."

Sidney Blakely only wanted to escape the coy, perfumed, primping, light-brained mass of calendar models at the Amoteh Resort.

She did not want to witness a suicide, a cliff jumper determined to end his miserable life.

On the other hand, as a professional photographer, she could get a good shot of—Sidney discarded that thought. For once, she didn't have a camera and she really didn't want to see someone splattered all over the rocks below. If he fell onto the sand, that might be different, but still—

She paused just a heartbeat—the man looked really big, maybe six foot three or so, and powerful. If she came too close, he could easily take her five-foot-five-inch, 110-pound body right over the cliff with him.

She might be Ben's sexual leftover, but she wasn't ready to die.

Sidney hurried to finish pulling on her camouflage pants and tugged her sweatshirt down to her hips. Her boots were discarded and she had no time to put them on before she stopped the jumper. The rocks bruised her feet as she tried to both hurry and avoid pain. "Ooh, ouch...ooh...ouch. Hey, mister. Don't do anything rash. Let's talk this—ouch—out."

Sidney came closer to stand a little behind the man—just out of reaching distance.

As a freelance photographer, she'd seen men, stunned by war, want to take their own lives. She'd seen them walk deliberately into enemy fire. She'd seen whole native villages taken out by floods and volcanoes; she'd captured the devastation of the western U.S. fires, flown above the scorching deserts, crossed desolate Arctic stretches to photograph reindeer herds. Well published in various magazines, she was an on-the-spot prime and well-paid photographer and she recognized people who were on the very edge of life, ready to throw it away.

This man was brooding, maybe contemplating death—she had to stay calm, work him down, make him see that life wasn't all that bad…even though hers was in the toilet now that Ben had married Fluffy.

She eased into position a few feet to the side of the "jumper," and studied him. The wind caught his hair, the salty mist swirling around him. Early thirties maybe, shaggy wavy hair, a rugged hard face and a jaw covered with stubble, from there on down, he was all power and broad shoulders and long lean legs in jeans that topped his work boots. The hand raised to push back his hair was big and wide and strong—he was a man who worked with his hands and those broad shoulders said he was probably a laborer, Sidney decided.

"I come up here to be alone," he whispered in a deep gravely voice.

Sidney moved closer. She had to think of something to keep him from jumping. "Yeah? Want to tell me why?"

He turned to her and those deep-set eyes, only slivers of silver in the night, pinned her. Oh, no, Sidney thought wildly, the guy could be a serial killer waiting here every night for his victim, and she'd walked right into—

A strand of his hair drifted across his cheekbone, softening the hard edge. His voice came deep and wrapped in a Western drawl that seemed to hold humor: "Sometimes, life is just the pits."

Sidney decided that serial killers probably weren't the humorous kind of guys and reverted back to her "jumper" theory. "How well I know—er, ah… Now, it isn't always the pits. Look at the bright side, guy. Why don't we talk about this?"

"What's 'this'?"

"You know, how good life is. We'll swap stories and you'll feel better. All we need is a beer and some talk and you'll see that life isn't that bad."

"'You brought beer up here?"

He sounded interested in that, but then maybe he was an alcoholic, and already pretty well on his way—but then he smelled like fresh air, newly cut lumber, that wonderful just showered soap-and-male smell. "No beer. Just a buddy to listen to you in the night. We'll swap stories. You'll see that my life is no joy ride and you'll feel better."

"I doubt if you can top what I'm going through."

"Oh, no, I can. Wait until I tell you about it—step back from the edge there and I'll tell you about my miserable excuse for a life. If you think you've got problems, you should try my life."

A human touch, that's what the man needed at his lowest hour, to know that someone cared about him. Sidney eased closer. "Now don't do anything rash, just take my hand."

His frown directed toward her was suspicious. "Why should I? What do you mean, rash?"

He wasn't playing his role well—she was supposed to be rescuing him and instead he was asking questions. "Because I said so, dammit. I mean that a step or two more and you could go over the edge."

He stared at her blankly for a moment and shook his head. "You think that I might— Uh…I see." In the darkness he smiled slightly, as if enjoying a new thought. "Okay," he agreed meekly.

He looked down at her extended hand, then slowly his large rough one closed over it. Calluses, Sidney thought, a workman who probably has pride in something—she just had to find out what made his life worth living and open the good things up for him.

Sidney inched back from the cliff and he followed her just those few feet. She breathed a little easier. Still. He could take a running jump at any time, and maybe take her with him. She could read the newspaper headlines now—or rather the memos and back copy that only a few people might read— Sidney Blakely, Freelance Photographer Dies in Lovers' Leap. Send donations to—yada, yada. Bulldog, her father, would curse her for stupid female brain and her sisters, Stretch and Junior, would be left to fend for themselves. Fluffy would cry prettily and Ben would yawn and turn over. He did that well, yawn and turn over when he finished sex— Well, sex with Fluffy now.

The problem was, this guy wasn't her lover. The headlines and memos would be wrong—typical bad reporting; the facts would be skewed.

"Guy, I'm going over there and sit down on my sleeping bag—" If the jumper was sitting, he couldn't jump, could he? "And you're welcome to sit a while. Or maybe we could walk down together. Maybe go for a beer somewhere?"

The man's palm fitted against hers, his fingers linked with hers. Oh—Sidney cursed mentally—he was going to take her over with him. She stepped up the pace, and tugged him along to the sleeping bag. "Sit, dammit."

"Are you always so sweet? That sounds like an order." There was a slight, but unusual accent in his voice. She couldn't place it—a cross between a Western drawl and something foreign.

"Bulldog—my dad was in the Marines. He raised my sisters and me according to regulations. Take it from there. And sit."

When the tall man folded himself down onto her sleeping bag, Sidney took a deep breath. Shoot, she knew a few self-defense moves and just where to hit a man where he was most vulnerable. She'd been in basic training and maneuvers since she was old enough to toddle. Besides, he was staring off to-

ward that cliff. It was probably calling him—jumpers sometimes said they got called to their deaths.

Sidney settled down on the sleeping bag, folded her legs
lotus-fashion, and tried to come up with something to quell
his suicide urges, something tender that he'd reflect upon and
change his mind. She came up with "You don't have a para-
chute. It would be messy at the bottom. You're big. Think of
the cleanup," she said.

He'd drawn up one knee, closed his arms around it. "Mmm.
I don't think I want to jump just yet. Maybe I wasn't going
to anyway. So what's the story of your life?"

Get personal, make an attachment, that's what Bulldog
had said about men who were weary of life. "Oh you had the
look all right. I've seen it in combat zones—sad, alone, as if
nothing else mattered... So, what's your name?"

"So, what's your story?"

She took a deep breath. "You're being difficult. One of
those. The name is Sid Blakely."

"Sid," he repeated softly, almost like a caress, with just that
lilt of accent. She stuck out her hand and he considered it before taking it, enfolding it with his large one. "Danya."

"Sounds foreign." Now she recognized that slight inflec-
tion. He was still shaking her hand, slowly, as though he were
studying the fit of it within his own. Just maybe he was wondering if he could drag her to the edge, and—

"Russian. My father and uncles immigrated, and I was
born here." He was looking at her hand in his, studying it.
"You have good hands. Working hands. Small."

Sidney withdrew her hand, but the feel of his remained—
warm, rough, big. She fought the little unexplained shiver that
shot through her. "Ah. See there. You have family. They probably worry about you. Think of them."

"Okay, I will. What's your story?"

"First, I want your promise that you won't jump off that
cliff after I tell you. Promise, and that's a direct order."

"Yes, sir."

She thought she heard humor in that tone, and then dismissed it. "That's better—Danya. You have a last name?"

"Stepanov."

"As in the Stepanov family who lives here? Mikhail, who manages the Amoteh Resort, and Stepanov as in Stepanov Furniture? But then you have a family here. I've heard about them, and they're hard to miss. You're not alone."

"I have just moved here last fall with my father, so that he can retire and relax near his brother—that is Fadey Stepanov, the owner of the furniture line. I've gone into business with my brother, Alexi. We're builders and remodelers." His smile was slow and thoughtful, as if he loved the ones who would go on living without him.... "Tell me your story. Maybe I can help you? Ships passing in the night and all that?"

She shook her head. "Keep the roles straight. I'm the one saving you, got it? You just go along and everything will be fine. You've got to realize that you're not alone, that's the first thing."

"But you are here with me—so I am not alone, is that not so? Are you always this bossy?"

Sidney frowned as she ran through her day in hell. "Like I said, it's been a rough day. I'm shooting a calendar, not my usual gig. I'm not into commercial portraits, but I wanted out of what I usually do—you know, to try something different. The pay is good, the work stinks—especially the off-hours when the models want to chum it up with me. We're staying at the Amoteh Resort, doing some beach shots, and at night, they want to play pajama party. They want to include me. I'm hiding out now. There's nothing worse than a bunch of women moaning over their boyfriends, talking lipstick and hair, and waxing their legs. You have no idea how bad that hurts. To shut them up, I let them do it…almost killed me. It doesn't stop at the legs, you know—they have to worry about their bikini lines. Now, that really hurts."

"Ouch."

Sidney nodded; Danya seemed to understand about bikini

pain. She could tell by his slight grimace. Communication was progressing; soon he would forget about jumping. She decided to find out the reason for his crossing-out-life-tonight gambit. Touching was always good, according to Bulldog, so Sidney reached out and patted Danya's jeaned thigh. It was hard and muscles tightened beneath her hand; Danya was in really good shape. He sucked in a breath and his hand had locked over hers, his thumb caressing her palm. It was probably because he needed human touch; Sidney allowed her hand to be held captive. "So, buddy, what's your story? I'm a good listener—at least, my boyfriend used to tell me that."

The mention of Ben took her backtracking to his choice of Fluffy, the blond bimbo, and Sidney was unfolding her whole miserable tale before she knew it. "His name was Ben. We'd been on a few photo shoots together, in some pretty tight places. I'd watch his back, he'd watch mine, that sort of thing. We camped together, went through land mines together, stood on the cusp of a lava river together, shooting away. It was great. He's a photojournalist. You may have seen our stuff in magazines. Though a lot of people really don't care about the photographer's credits."

"And?" He rubbed her hand slowly up and down his thigh, but then, she justified, the guy probably had a muscle ache.

"And sex. We had that—oh, maybe twice a year…when there was time. Nothing like whole hours or anything—you just don't play around when you're out there shooting stuff. You get the job done and go on. So, anyway, we had a thing going for oh, six or seven years, and then he meets Fluffy-baby. They got married a month ago. That's why I don't want to take any freelance jobs where I might cross paths with Ben. Fluffy-baby hangs all over him. It's disgusting."

"I see," Danya said softly. "So that would hurt you?"

"It would make me mad. Fluffy hadn't got a thing to offer. Some little sweetie pie who hasn't been anywhere or done anything, but that isn't bad—it's just that we had done all those great, exciting things together and then he up and dumps me for her."

Sidney lay back on the sleeping bag and her hand was released. As the wind riffled her hair almost playfully, she inhaled the damp scents of night, mingled with the earth and trees. A short distance away, a small animal rustled through the underbrush, and she carefully moved through memories before speaking. "Bulldog never liked Ben. So at least I don't have to listen to lectures from sweet old Dad anymore."

Grass brushed her feet and clung to them. She kicked slightly to dislodge the damp blades, and he noted the action. "Did you hurt your feet when you walked over the rocks?"

Danya reached to take her foot and draw it into his hands. He smoothed her arch and insole very slowly. A woman who knew how to take what she could get in a single moment of life, because it could be gone the next, Sidney relaxed slightly. She wanted to give him something back. "Hey, want a candy bar?" she asked as she dug into her pants cargo pocket.

"No, thanks." He carefully drew off her thick workman's sock, and continued to slowly, carefully rub her feet.

Sidney unwrapped the chocolate bar and munched on it, contemplating Ben's defection while having her feet warmed and soothed. "I loved him—Ben, I mean. We shared film and lenses and hardships. A thing like that doesn't go away easy. Now he's with her, the six-foot-nothing-but-legs-and-boobs blond bimbo. I don't know what he sees in her. They are planning to multiply and raise ducks. He's all excited, Mr. Rabbit, so fast you never know he's been there before he's gone. Now, I've got a reason to jump off that—er, to eat a lot of these candy bars."

She plopped her other foot into his hands. "Do that one. Talk. Pick up the pace."

His hands moved slowly, carefully over her feet; his voice was husky and uneven. His thumbs cruised over her arches. "You've got small feet."

She hoped he wasn't getting ready to cry. She didn't know how to handle tears, not even her own. Right now, thinking about Ben and Fluffy, Sidney's eyes were burning. But a

Blakely never cries. Bulldog would be shamed. That was why she carried the candy bars and why she'd put on weight— whenever she started to tear up, she'd grab something chocolate and focus on that. "Yeah. Hard to get the right kind of combat boots for my size, but I'm wearing hiking ones now. So what's your story?"

"My wife died in a car wreck. I was driving," he said simply.

Sidney swallowed the bite of chocolate. "You feel guilty."

"Because I lived and she didn't. A drunken driver met us head-on and crossed in front of us at the last minute. I didn't come to for days, and when I did—Jeannie was gone. We were both twenty-three."

"That's a heavy load. When did it happen?"

"Nine years ago. I still see those headlights…every night when I close my eyes." Danya lay down, put his hands behind his head and stared at the night sky.

"Wow. And I thought I had it bad." The companionable thing to do would be to lie quietly and wait for him to talk, so that's what Sidney did. She had to lie close because it was a single sleeping bag.

She needed to distract him from his grief and refocus him on something else. "I detest being closeted every day and night with these models. I'll be glad when this gig is over. They won't leave me alone. I'm just not into girly talk and she-she."

"You could stay somewhere else." He reached for her free hand and eased it beneath his shirt. The poor guy needed human touch, she thought as he rubbed her hand over his muscled stomach, and he felt good to touch, she decided.

"Do you ache—I mean, do you have some physical problem that might cause you to want to end it all? If you do, there are all sorts of counselors for pain—and for grief, by the way. Have you tried that?"

"No to the second part, but yes, now I do ache. Your hand feels good. Do you mind?"

"Not if it helps you. I've done massage when needed. I've

been in lots of make-do situations, and most of the time it's just people helping people, letting them know that someone cares. But I would sure like to escape those models. That's why I brought my sleeping bag up here—to get away from them since there's nowhere else to stay besides my room at Amoteh. Where are you staying? With your family?"

"In my family's cabin along the beach. It's quiet, private, except for the wind chimes and the waves. It's pretty plain, one room, no luxuries like at the Amoteh Resort."

"Sounds like heaven."

The mist had turned to a gentle rain and Sidney knew she couldn't stay all night—a photographer with a bad cold could ruin a shoot. Then she sneezed. "Look, I've got to go. Come down off this hill with me? We'll go someplace for a beer and talk some more."

"Everything is closed."

"We could go to my room and raid the refrigerator there, but those models would be on you like flies on sugar. They're man-hungry and you're in no emotional shape to fight them off. They're already half mad at me, so I'd have to let them have you—for the sake of the shoot. Now, you wouldn't want that, would you? A bunch of sex-starved, booby bimbos chasing you?"

He chuckled softly, deeply in the night. "No, I sure wouldn't want that."

At least his humor was there. Maybe she had done some good after all. Sidney sat up and looked for her socks. Danya took her foot and slowly slid one sock on and then the other. Sidney had the strangest sense that she was being tended somehow.

It was a gentle, but uneasy sensation that caused her to jam on her hiking boots and lace them tightly. "You want to talk at your place, or what?" she asked abruptly as she stood. "If not, then I'm going to have to go back into that bimbo hell and try to find a quiet corner where someone isn't sobbing over some girly movie, or someone isn't wanting to give me a facial or pluck my eyebrows. The light won't be good for shooting tomorrow, so they know they can stay up late—hunting me."

He handed her the sports bra and her cotton briefs. There was nothing intimate about it, only one buddy helping another. She stuffed them into her sleeping bag and Danya stood. He bent down to roll her bag and lift it over his shoulder. "Let's go."

"I can carry that. Who do you think waits on me?"

"I don't doubt it a bit. It's just that you've helped me tonight, and I'd like to return the favor…so I wouldn't be in your debt. You understand."

Sidney did understand. She never liked to be in anyone's debt and Bulldog had taught her to be self-sufficient. But if Danya needed that link to keep him off that cliff, she could sacrifice. He carefully led her down the rocky trail from the chieftain's grave site. Around her smaller one, his hand felt good, strong, and companionable. Maybe he needed that link with her. Maybe she needed it with him. Ships in the night, Sidney reminded herself. At least she wasn't at the mercy of the models.

Danya held her hand as they walked in the night, down Strawberry Hill and a long walk to the Amoteh Resort's steps. From there, they moved across a small worn path and down to the shoreline and Amoteh, the town. In the distance behind them, a huge jagged rock jutted up into the night, the waves crashing around it; she recognized the landmark as Deadman's Rock where boats had been smashed upon the rock and people had died.

She glanced at the man whom she had rescued. He looked big and lethal, hard and soulless, the wind catching his hair. He kept on one side of her, breaking the wind, and handling her sleeping bag as if it were nothing. Sidney hurried to match his long stride, but then she noted that it had shortened, and that he moved with her. She only reached his shoulder, her hand small within his.

The guy was a toucher, needing and giving touches and she could handle that—if it would help him deal with his pain. She'd talk him through the night and in the morning, he'd feel much better.

They passed docking piers, the boats moving in the waves, gently bumping at their moorings, then the long tourist pier filled with shops that were now closed, flags trembling above them.

Then, just as they passed a long margin of driftwood piled on the shore, Sidney decided that maybe Danya really only needed to have sex to make him see that life was worth living.

But not with her. She stopped, jerked her hand away from his, and plopped down on a log. "Wait a minute. Wait a minute—"

Danya loomed above her, the sleeping bag propped over his shoulder. "Problem?"

"I just want to get something straight. No sex. No way. Not with me. You've got to promise to think of me as a friend, a buddy, not a woman." She patted a driftwood log. "Sit."

"I do not think of you as just a woman," Danya said slowly, thoughtfully, with that touch of foreign formality.

He eased down to the log and studied her, his face all angles in the mist and eery moonlight. "Good. Just keep thinking of me as your buddy and we'll be fine. Men usually think of me that way and I'm used to talking straight with them, no female chatter for me. Do you have a sexual problem? Because if you do, I can't help you there."

Was he trying not to smile? "Not that I know of."

"What's your sexual history? I'm just asking because I don't want to be jumped by some guy with stored up—some guy needing relief. I mean, have you done it since your wife—you know?"

"A few times. But I didn't find what my wife and I had and I needed that to feel complete."

"No offense, but you understand why I need to be careful."

"You have my word that I will not touch you—like that. But it is nice to listen to you talk. If you would stay with me, it would fill the hours."

She eyed him and could find no humor in that hard face. "Are you saying that I talk too much? Because I'm just trying to help you, after all."

"I am saying that I would be pleased if you would share my home tonight." Again, his formality caused Sidney to be uneasy. But then, she'd met a few European males and though this guy was born in the U.S., sometimes family traditions carried over; he probably even spoke Russian. She'd noticed that same formality in Mikhail Stepanov, and a slight disdain for the models hovering around him.

"I'm not having sex with you—just getting that straight upfront. Been there, done that, with Mr. Rabbit, and it wasn't fun. What happened to these other women you've had?"

Danya looked out to the black waves. "Correction—a couple of women, each for a brief time. It seems that I am a good matchmaker. Through me, they met someone more suitable than myself."

"Oh, that's too bad. So you were dumped. Danya, you can't think of yourself as a life's loser just because you were dumped."

"That is good advice. I'm tired and my cabin is just a little bit farther. Do you want to go on, or back to the resort?"

Sidney yawned and thought of the primping models waiting to give her facials, pluck her eyebrows, share intimate girl-talk and discuss silly fashions. "If I could pull up a piece of your floor for my sleeping bag, I'd be grateful."

He nodded and stood. Exhausted now, Sidney yawned again and looked down at the big hand extended to help her to her feet.

Bulldog wouldn't like her accepting help, but since this guy needed lots of touching to get him through the night, what did it matter?

In her lifetime, Sidney had had to make quick decisions and always trusted her judgment. Now it told her that she could trust this man. He needed companionship for the night and she needed rest.

It would all work out, she decided as she walked with him to his cabin.

And then her artistic photographer's mind added an enticing thought—he was gorgeous and just maybe she could get some really good shots, a portrait in black and white would really emphasize that rugged face.

That long lean body wasn't that bad, either, she decided, and it would be perfect for some excellent shots, maybe for magazine ads. She might even be a factor in changing his life, in starting him in new successful directions, in giving him a new and beautiful slant on life.

Hey, when opportunity raised its beautiful, profitable head, who was she to deny it?

Two

Sidney Blakely fascinated Danya; every sensual molecule in his body had fastened onto that small curvaceous body.

He really should feel guilty—after all, if he hadn't been enjoying her so much, he would have worked harder to correct her "jumper" image of him. But the need to explore Sidney Blakely more was too irresistible to ignore.

She had absolutely no idea how appealing she was, nor how she had aroused him…he concluded as she mounted the steps to the cabin ahead of him.

His hands ached to cup her bottom, to feel that softness, as the scent of her tightened every muscle in his body. The immediate need to stake his claim on this woman surprised him.

She was not wearing any underclothing.

On the cabin porch, she looked around to see the wind chimes made of spoons, and a delicate fingertip reached to toy with them. A woman who had lived with men, communicated on their no-nonsense level, Sidney liked to keep her options open. "I could sleep right here, listening to the ocean."

He wanted her in his bed—now. "It will rain soon. You'll keep drier inside, and you could sleep in—if you're not shooting tomorrow."

"Oh, that sounds so good. I've been missing sleep."

He understood perfectly; Sidney had come to Kamakani's grave site to discuss her ill-fated love for "Mr. Rabbit."

Danya thought of making slow, soft love to her, of waking up to her and moving into her, and his body tightened painfully. *After all these years of emptiness, why this special woman? Why tonight?*

Inside the cabin, Sidney looked around at the Spartan furnishings—the big solid Stepanov bed and dresser, a plain table and two chairs, a kitchenette. She walked to the tiny bathroom and peeked inside. "Great," she stated approvingly.

"Sid?" Danya unfurled her sleeping bag and placed it against a corner of the room. He could see her plainly now, the practical short hair cut. Her eyes were dark brown and large, almost like a fawn's, her lashes sweeping shadows down that pale soft skin. She wore no cosmetics, and he ached to taste that slender throat, to nibble on those small ears.

His body knew it had been years since he'd made love to a woman, awakening now to the twin peaks of her breasts, nudging the heavy sweatshirt.

"Yeah?" She was stretching and yawning and Danya ached to hold that small shapely body tight against him. She rotated her head and bent to touch her toes several times and the cargo pants tightened over her curved backside.

He ached to be inside, filling her—

"I thought you might like this." He reached down to a laundry basket on the floor and pulled out a folded T-shirt, tossing it to her.

Sidney came close to study the framed picture on the dresser, a young Danya and his bride, just after their wedding. "I'm so sorry," she said, reaching to touch his back and when she looked up at him, her eyes spoke more than words. "She's beautiful."

"Yes, very beautiful. A treasure of the heart. I will keep her always there," he said solemnly, meaning it.

"That's beautiful, Danya. But you've got to live your life. If I go to sleep, you won't do anything rash, will you?"

He shook his head. "I'm too tired. Emotions, you know. I don't suppose you could—no...I won't ask."

Danya almost felt guilty—but not quite as Sidney's expressive eyes filled with him. "What, Danya?"

"Could I hold you?"

Instantly she was alert and stepping back warily from him. "Whoa, champ. I'm *not* the girl you want."

She was exactly the woman he wanted. "Sorry. I get the need sometimes to hold a woman. Just hold her, and I don't know why, but women get ideas and the next thing you know—"

She seemed to relax. "Human touch, right?"

Sidney stepped closer with the determined air of one who is sacrificing. "Hold me. Do it, now. You've got thirty seconds."

Danya eased her against him, rested his chin over hers, and inhaled her fragrance and closed his eyes, focusing on the fit, the feel of her in his arms. Inside, where his heart had been cold and hurt, the warmth of pleasure and delight began—

"Time's over," Sidney said, pushing away.

He forced himself to release her. "Thanks. I feel better now."

"Yeah, well." She cleared her throat and backed away, her expression wary as she bent to collect her things. She turned and hurried into the bathroom.

Danya rubbed his stubble-covered jaw. At three o'clock in the morning, there was nothing he wanted to do more than cuddle Sidney Blakely. With a sigh, Danya turned off the lights, undressed and slid into his lonely bed.

Inside the bathroom, Sidney quickly undressed and slid on her comfortable boxer shorts and Danya's overlarge T-shirt. She was shaking.

She'd wanted to nail him, to stake him out on that big bed and have him. Sexual impulses didn't come to her often—

maybe never. Sex with Ben, her only lover to date, had been too fast and had left her simmering.

The poor guy was thinking about suicide and mourning his wife, and Sidney was thinking about how good he felt up close and that just maybe she might get a good photo layout of him. She was scum to even think about nabbing him and curling up to that nice big hard warm body— She shook her head. There was no way she would take advantage of a sweet man like that, using him for her own satisfaction.

She was just tired and emotional, she decided as she left the bathroom and found the main room dark and cozy. A pillow and a sheet lay on her sleeping bag and it looked like heaven.

Danya's broad back was turned to her and Sidney spread the sheet over the bag, slid onto it, and folded the rest of the sheet over her. She punched the pillow into shape and with the ease of someone who took what she could get on the spot, quickly dropped into sleep.

Danya listened to her deep easy breathing and turned to look at the slight, curved shadow on the floor. The sheet had slid from her bare leg and her hands were up by her face, almost like a child's.

He eased from his bed and walked to crouch and study the woman who had no idea how much she fascinated him…. Her lips were generous and soft, slightly parted; her lashes swept shadows down that fine pale skin.

A compassionate woman, she'd endangered herself to rescue someone she thought might leap to his death. Unfamiliar with caresses or letting her body rest against a man's, she'd still let him hold her; she'd touched him because she thought he needed the warmth of another human.

But on the rebound, Sidney wasn't in the market for romance, and that was just what Danya had in mind.

It would take all his willpower to treat her as a friend, when he really wanted to make love with her. He scanned the curved line of her body beneath the sheet, his hand aching to skim that warmth.

Very little kept him from carrying her to his bed, where she belonged; very little kept him from holding her safe and warm, to cherish her.

To move into a relationship with this brusque, but caring woman, would be no easy task. She'd been wounded by a former lover and was wary of men, but Danya intended to be very patient and he intended to have her as his own....

Sidney awoke to the scent of coffee and the sight of Danya, holding a cup and staring off into the morning rain battering the cabin's window. He wore only his jeans, his back broad and tanned in the dim light. The pose, the blend of shadow and light would have been wonderful for a photograph, that waving hair softening his hard profile, that jaw darkened by stubble. He looked thoughtful, grim and fierce.

"So how's it going, buddy?" Sidney asked after yawning and stretching. "Feeling better?"

Apparently still deep in thought, he nodded. Sidney rose to her feet, shuffled to the kitchenette to pour herself a cup of coffee. She took a sweet roll from the plastic container, and walked to stand beside him. "Thanks for last night...letting me crash here, I mean."

"Sure."

Rain pounded the windows, the dim light outside casting shadows on Danya's hard face; his mood seemed to match the elements outside. "Are you going to be okay today?"

"Yes. Alexi and I are remodeling, adding a family room onto a house. You can stay here, if you want, Sid. I mean, you can move in with me, if you want, to escape those models. It's up to you. But there could be gossip. People might think that we were lovers."

She studied the shadows beneath his eyes, the look of a man who had been through hell, who had been on some invisible edge, fighting the tethers that bound him. "I've bunked with men before."

Danya inhaled suddenly, then released his breath slowly. He looked at her and his eyes were the color of blue ice. "This is different. I don't want you to have problems."

She'd heard that the Stepanov males were very gallant, but manners and female-male role playing weren't for her; they just cluttered up life and took time she didn't have. "The only problem I am going to have is that darned windup dance and social thingie at the end of this shoot. Marvelous Calendars insists on it. All the bigwigs are going to come down and I've got orders to look like a woman—put on a dress and makeup and everything. I'm supposed to bring a date."

"That is rough."

"Real rough. You'd think if I do a good job—and I do— that would be all that was required, but oh, no. I have to mix with the brass and schmooze with the models and be one of the girls. I am going to have to dance with the execs—in dress shoes, not boots."

"Torture," he agreed softly.

"You know it. If the weather clears, we've got about two, three days fast shooting and then I'm doomed." Sidney yawned and stretched and settled into enjoy her momentary reprieve from the models. She ate the sweet roll and sipped her coffee, then she licked her fingers. Danya had been studying her intensely and his body was tense next to hers; his breathing seemed to be controlled, rather than natural. She'd been remiss not to offer him a bite; she was used to sharing whatever was at hand. "Want some?" she asked, holding up her sweet roll to him.

His hand wrapped around her wrist as he bent to take a bite, but his eyes never left hers. They were vividly blue and shadowed with heavy lashes. He straightened, still studying her, his thumb caressing her inner wrist. "About Ben. You loved him?"

Sidney was uncomfortable with that slow caress, but if the guy needed contact, she could give him that. "I still do, the rat. I'm going back to bed, if it's okay with you."

"My bed," he said quietly, watching her. "I'll be gone. You might as well use it. You've got sugar on your fingers—shame to waste it."

Sidney watched, riveted as Danya's dark head bent and his warm mouth closed over each fingertip, sucking it.

The quivery sensations shot up her arm and down her body to lodge low in her belly; her mouth dried and her throat tightened as she stared at him. When Danya's head lifted, he smiled at her and her heart did some flip-flop thing. "No finger licking," she said unevenly.

"But it would be a shame to waste, would it not?" His voice was deep and intimate, his phrasing formal.

"I guess it's okay this time."

Danya had kept her hand, holding it as they turned to watch the dim morning, rain slashing the windows.

Sidney held very still. She was very aware of him, of how large his body was to hers, of his body heat, of his hand, rough against hers. "So, chum. Are you going to be okay today? I mean, if I go to sleep, will you be okay?"

"Of course. I have work to do. Work is good. You are welcome here."

"Thanks. Maybe I will sleep in. A good morning for that."

He seemed to tense, and those blue eyes flashed down at her. "Yes," Danya said unevenly, "A very good morning for staying in bed."

Danya tried to focus on the cabinets his brother and he were installing into the family room addition, but his mind was on Sidney—lying in his bed.

At three o'clock in the afternoon, the day was clearing, and he'd already had several calls on his cell phone from his obviously amused family—Sidney had seemed concerned for him and was hunting him. She'd been to the Stepanov Furniture factory, talked with Fadey and Viktor, Danya's father, who had found her to be fresh and delightful. She'd taken pictures of Fadey and Viktor in a spirited folk dance, and she'd joined them in it. Danya's father said he had hugged her—a traditional big bear hug, kissing both sides of her cheeks, and "she felt like a sweet little bird in his arms, before she squirmed away."

According to Mikhail's report, she'd worked in her suite at the Amoteh Resort, requesting a sandwich from room service. Alexi's cell phone had rung several times, and from his brother's expression, Danya knew that the entire family was watching the "Sidney situation." She had been careful to ask that someone was with him and to pinpoint his quitting time. She'd murmured something obscure, "He's a lonely kind of guy. I really don't think he should be left alone."

Mikhail and Jarek, Danya's cousins, were sitting on sawhorses now, using the excuse of a coffee break to come to the remodeling project. Apparently their wives were seeking information about the woman Danya had brought back to his cabin, and needed their husbands to scout for information. Danya didn't want the whole Stepanov clan to descend upon Sidney, frightening her away. "She is…unusual…sweet…and completely unaware that she is so—feminine and fascinating. She considers us to be buddies. I prefer to keep it that way."

"Of course," Mikhail agreed firmly. "I've met her. She's fast moving, thorough, and completely professional. She doesn't want a man opening a door for her, but she will open them for a man—quite unusual woman, eats on the run and seems in perpetual motion. The models like her, but she doesn't want any 'hugging, sloppy stuff,' as she says. She strikes me as a person who is more of an observer of life, rather than one who actually lives with day-to-day relationships."

"Not a clue that you want her, hmm?" Jarek asked.

"She's just been hurt by man who married someone else. I met her up on Strawberry Hill last night and she needed a place to stay away from the resort. I intend to give her time to adjust to a comfortable relationship."

Alexi grinned broadly. "So this is it, huh?"

"Maybe." Danya glanced at a movement outside the windows and noted Sidney tramping along the shoreline, dressed in her camouflage cargo pants and hooded jacket, a camera bag slung from her shoulder. She stopped, faced the ocean and quickly, expertly, extracted her large camera from the bag. Her movements on the beach said that she was shooting pictures.

Alexi, Mikhail and Jarek came to stand beside Danya. "I think she's coming to collect you," Alexi stated with humor in his tone.

"If she asked your quitting time, that's a possibility," Mikhail noted.

Danya watched that small taut body, poised against sand and ocean and forced himself to breathe quietly, though his heart was quickening and his body had tensed, eager for her to come to him.

"You're getting that definite hot-and-bothered look, cousin," Jarek added with a chuckle.

"Say anything about that, and you won't be invited to the wedding." Danya folded his arms and leveled a look at his brother and cousins. "Tell your wives this is a very tricky situation. Sidney hasn't a clue. I would appreciate their cooperation."

Alexi shook his head. "You mean, you want our wives to keep their distance, as if that's possible. They've been worrying about you for months now, since you moved and they got you under their wings. You scooped them, cousin, found your own woman and that leaves them with little to do."

Danya picked a baby rattle from Alexi's pocket and shook it lightly. "Your wife had a baby, Jarek has two, and Mikhail has three. I would say that is enough to keep them busy…just for a time. Please ask them."

Mikhail drew a deep breath. "It might not be possible to stop them. They're having tea at my house now."

"Sidney isn't the tea and sewing kind. I've asked her to move in with me. I'll baby-sit for a week apiece if you can keep them off her for just a bit. Think of a holiday alone with your wives."

Jarek whistled softly. "Fast work."

"Put your feet down. Make your wives toe the line, men," Danya added with a chuckle. "As if you could. You're all wrapped up around their little fingers."

"Just wait, cousin," Mikhail warned with a grin and glanced out of the window. "She's getting closer."

The four men watched Sidney march up the shoreline toward the house; they hurried to act busy.

No one answered her knock at the new door, but Sidney could hear saws buzzing. She noted the fresh scent of lumber, the Stepanov Building pickup parked at one end of the private home. The barren new windows and new door marked the new addition.

She opened the door, scanned the jumble of tools and working men and waited for someone to notice her. When the men continued working and the saw didn't stop, she yelled, "Danya!"

When he didn't respond, she decided he couldn't hear her over the sound of the saw and hammers. Sidney opened the door wider and peered inside. The four tall men continued to work. She stepped inside and closed the door. Amid the flying sawdust, Danya was standing on a ladder, fitting a shelf into a built-in ceiling-to-floor bookcase.

The man at the table saw noted her and flipped it off. He removed his safety glasses, and his eyes were as blue as Danya's. "Yes?" he asked politely.

Danya was hammering the board into place. The other two men were working together, putting up dry wall panels.

"Is Danya Stepanov here?" Sidney asked the blue-eyed man politely. His rugged face was similar to Danya's, but then so were the other men's. She already knew that Danya was there, because his butt was fine and taut within his jeans and she couldn't take her eyes off it. She itched to use her camera; she could just imagine how much a magazine would pay for that...or maybe that broad muscled back, without his shirt, of course. Who was she kidding? Pictures weren't on her mind; she just wanted to run her hands over that back and butt and maybe other things, too. She usually methodically considered the specific shot, focusing on the shadows, the angles, backgrounds—but now, her whole body was considering the very touchable textures of the man.

"He is busy."

"I see that. I want to talk with him."

"It's only a little while until quitting. If you're his girlfriend, you'll have to wait."

"Listen, Bud. I'm not his girlfriend, I just want to talk with him." Sidney never wasted time. She walked to Danya, who seemed very intent on his work and yelled, "Danya, get your butt down here. I want to talk with you."

He seemed surprised as he turned to look down at her. "Oh…hi, Sid. What's up?"

She noted that all of a sudden, the three other men were watching her. She moved closer so that they wouldn't hear the conversation. She had to stand on tiptoe to whisper in Danya's ear. He leaned down to her, and his hands rested lightly on her waist. His hands were big and firm and something inside her shimmered and warmed.

"Are you okay?" she asked, remembering how they met on Strawberry Hill, how he seemed to need to touch, to anchor himself to her and to life.

"I am fine," he whispered back.

"Is that offer to move into your place still standing? It's so quiet there. I slept like a log until after noon. I can use the resort's suite for my work, so I won't clutter up your place with my equipment."

"The models again?"

Sidney tried not to look hunted. "They're getting all warmed up for that party I don't want to go to…. I'd pay rent."

Danya frowned. "You insult me. You gave me comfort last night, and you think I would want pay?"

He was very close and scented of fresh wood. "So you're okay with this? Is tonight okay?"

His gaze took in her face. "Tonight is excellent."

Sidney realized that his hands were tightening, drawing her closer to him. His face was only inches from hers—probably better to hear her whisper. "What about your family? Will they mind?"

"No, I assure you, they will be most happy that you are with me."

"Good."

Danya turned her slowly in front of him, his hands still resting on her waist. "This is Alexi, my brother...my cousins, Jarek and Mikhail. Perhaps you have met Mikhail? This is Sidney Blakely. She's the photographer for the models here."

"Call me Sid." She recognized the manager of the luxurious Amoteh Resort. In work clothing, he looked so different from the sleek businessman striding through the resort's halls and expertly, quietly directing his staff. "Hi, Mikhail. Nice to meet you, guys. I'm just leaving. You can get back to work now."

But each man came close, towering over her. They looked so much alike, but Mikhail's and Jarek's eyes were dark green, while Alexi's eyes were as blue as Danya's. Smaller than the men by several inches, Sidney glared up at them. "You guys should take better care of Danya," she scolded.

"Oh, how so?" Alexi said as he frowned down at her.

"He's a lonely sort of guy. Like tonight. I bet you could all invite him over to dinner, and you probably haven't, right?"

The three men glanced over her head to Danya, seemed to be amused, then they shook their heads. "You are right," Alexi said, "We forget about him at times."

"I guess we are so comfortable in our own homes with our families that we forget he might need us," Jarek murmured contritely.

"Shame on you," Sidney scolded. "That is not very familylike."

"You are absolutely right, Sid. How thoughtless of us," Mikhail said firmly.

Sidney realized that she was holding Danya's hand, his

thumb caressing the back of hers. His other arm had gone around her, resting lightly on her waist. She seemed to fit naturally into the cove of his body as he drew her close and looked down at her. "Actually, Sid, it isn't their fault. It's mine. I'm kind of a loner. Sid, do you think I could cook something for us tonight—you and me, I mean?"

She frowned at his selfish family, who hadn't thought to include him in their warmth, a guy who needed someone to keep him from that dangerous edge. His defense of them was just loyalty. "Sure. You do that. See you later."

Sidney moved toward the door and Danya came to open it for her. "I can do that for myself," she said. "I'm not helpless."

"Of course. I should have known. I'll come outside with you."

Sidney opened the door, Danya went through it and she leveled a look at the three other tall men. "I thought I heard a laugh. What's so funny?"

All three men held up their hands, their expressions innocent.

"Okay, then. At ease, men," Sidney said and closed the door.

Danya was waiting for her, and his eyes were as blue as the clear sky. For a moment, Sidney's mind went blank and she struggled to comprehend what he was saying: "What are you hungry for?"

"Whatever. You don't have to cook though. Sandwiches are good. I'll bring some home."

"No. I will cook for you."

Sidney took a deep breath and released the thought that had been hovering in her mind: "Danya, I know it is a lot to ask, but do you think you could turn up at the…the windup party and maybe act like you're my date?"

"I would be honored."

"Now, look. You don't have to. You don't owe me anything—"

"Sid. You can count on me," he said firmly. "See you tonight. Whenever you come home is okay, no big deal."

Relieved that she had found the required date, Sidney

walked back up to the Amoteh Resort. Plus, she added, she was really doing Danya a favor by keeping his mind away from jumping off that cliff. She would at least have her nights free—no more models, no more threats of bikini waxes and eyebrow plucking, no sex stories.

The sky was clear now, children playing along the shoreline, tourists milling on the pier filled with shops, a sailboat lazily riding the waves.

One of the models nabbed her when she entered the resort's pool area. Lelani Berry was a six-foot lithesome blonde, wearing two scraps that served as a bikini over her tanned, pampered body. Her expensively streaked long hair was perfectly tousled as she asked, "Hey, Sid, what are you wearing to the party?"

Then came the slow, sultry smile that hid a viperous mentality. "The next question is, who is your date? I heard you'd been ordered to bring one."

"Got a date. Don't know what I'm wearing." Sidney maneuvered through the cluster of lounging chairs, draped with model bodies.

She almost made it through the gauntlet, when Storm Cameron, also six feet tall with a blond mane, caught her. "So, Sid. Who is he?"

Miss January, a hot-looking Latino model with masses of raven hair blocked Sidney's passage to the hallway. Jennifer Mendez leaned against the wall and tapped her long painted nails on her cheek. "You're going to need help, Shorty," she said in her Bronx accent. "Dress, heels, that sort of thing. We've got our work cut out for us, ladies."

Sidney shot her a dark look and then turned to the rest of the models who looked excited and ready to mob her. "Hands off. If anyone nags me about this, I swear I'll shoot your bad sides and make you look like hags. I make notes, you know… for the calendar guys, on who was difficult and who wasn't, just so they know who not to hire next time."

A ripple of fear shot through the models and for a moment,

Sidney felt guilty; they were just making a living, the same as her. Lelani Berry had had a really hard life, and was driven to succeed; she just needed someone to help her understand that survival didn't depend on slash and burn methods. Sidney decided that when she could, she'd try to explain that fact to Lelani.

"Okay, everybody on the beach, just as you are. The light isn't that great, but not that bad either. We'll do the shoot and let the graphic guys worry about what works. Wear something over your suits, no topless stuff, and we'll take a few sunset shots. You've got an hour to get yourself camera ready, bring towels—we're shooting on driftwood. Tell Earl to bring some glitter."

Earl, the Hollywood makeup man contracted for this job, was good and he knew it. And when Sidney, moving fast, had become impatient and had called him a prima donna, he'd retaliated by making her say "Please, Earl" to get the smallest service.

If Earl wasn't balking now over some itty-bitty statement she'd made like "Move your butt, Earl," she had just an hour to get her stuff moved down to Danya's cabin—maybe more, because the models always took more time than allowed....

On her way out of the Amotch's side door, she met Mikhail Stepanov. She slung her duffel bag over her shoulder and opened the door for him and held it. "Well, get in. I don't have all day."

He hesitated, then entered and said formally, "Thank you."

"Yeah, sure. Whatever."

She hurried out and down the resort steps, picked up a back trail that looked as if it would lead to Danya's cabin on the shoreline and hurried over it.

She had just reached his cabin's steps when she saw them— On the beach, three big men were wrestling, rolling in the sand and grunting. The men's bodies thrashed and buckled into a big ball of muscle and she recognized Danya on the bottom— Sidney dropped her duffel bag and hurried to the men. "Get off him," she ordered, but the grunting, rolling male mass continued.

Experienced with men displaying machismo and as the fight-settler between Stretch and Junior, her tall, athletic sisters, Sidney wasted no time in acting. She grabbed the ear of one man and one ear of the other. "Didn't you hear my order, men? I said 'get off him.'"

"Ouch…ouch…"

She eased them away from Danya who was at the bottom of the pile. He smiled sheepishly. "Thanks."

He rose to his feet and she briskly dusted the sand from his clothing. He frowned slightly and looked at the other men. "Turn," she said and Danya looked at her warily, so she moved around him and dusted sand from that taut backside. Then, she faced the men, her hands on her hips. "Well, what do you have to say for yourselves? First, you don't share what you have with the guy, and then you mob him. Speak up. Say something. Do it now."

Alexi and Jarek were rubbing their ears and glaring at Danya. "Sorry?" they asked angrily in unison without the slightest hint of an apology.

"What's this all about, men?" she demanded. "Cut the excuses."

"Teasing…they were teasing me," Danya said softly. "We have wrestled like this since we were children."

Now she felt embarrassed; they were just playing as men do, as she and her sisters did sometimes. "Oh. I see."

Danya's blue eyes seemed to fill with her, to absorb her. The salty air seemed to shift a little, heat and still, and the crashing of the waves seemed to be inside her heart—

"Well, boys, now that's settled, I've got a shoot in a little bit," Sidney stated briskly as pulled herself out of whatever was happening between Danya and herself. She hurried to collect her duffel bag and place it in the house. She dug out her camera gear and wished she didn't have to face the men.

Danya entered the cabin, and because she'd misunderstood

the situation, and because men sometimes got all huffy when a woman rescued them, Sidney said, "Um…sorry about that."

He stripped off his shirt and tossed it into a hamper. "About what?"

"About butting in. Got to go. See you later." The sight of his chest, all muscled and tanned and the peaks of his nipples on those rounded pecs caused her throat to dry. She ached to rummage her fingers through that wedge of hair on his chest and maybe follow that thin line downward—

She hurried out the door because in another minute, she'd be reaching to touch him.

The models were clustering on the beach, oiling themselves and reapplying makeup, tousling their hair, and Sidney gave herself to the artistry of nature and female form, the blend of light and water and wind. As usual, a small crowd had collected, watching her work.

When the light was almost gone, Sidney let the models go with an order to get plenty of sleep because they were shooting all the next day.

She sat on a driftwood log and relaxed, a peaceful moment by herself after a heavy concentration of arranging limbs and hair and best sides, and the continual suggestions and grumbling. Earl could be temperamental and she'd had to force herself to heap praise upon him—after he had balked at something minor she'd said like "Move your butt, Earl. I'm losing light."

Danya came to sit beside her. "Tired?"

"Beat is more like it. There's a lot of emotion in this, getting the right shot, working with models. I'd prefer natural shots, but this gig was pretty high paying. Plus, I didn't want to meet up with Ben anywhere. Fluffy would be hanging all over him." She caught the scent of soap and man and looked at him. "Are you okay?"

"Sure. Dinner is ready when you are."

Preparing dinner probably kept Danya busy and his mind off his lost love. They watched the setting sun, the bright border of orange on the horizon. The waves slid softly upon the sand and Sidney sighed tiredly. "Ben would have liked this."

"Mr. Rabbit?"

In the comradery of the moment, Sidney shared an insight with him. "His fast moves could have been my fault. There's a lot of articles written about what pleases a man. I wouldn't buy something like that…I get complimentary magazine copies because of my work for the publishers. I just didn't take time to read them. I've always been pretty capable."

"Sure." He sounded disbelieving.

She eyed him. "You don't believe me?"

He riffled her hair playfully. "Sure I do."

"I could have done a lot better than you did out there in the sand today."

Danya seemed to smirk. "I don't think so. You're small."

"Oh, you don't, do you?" Sidney stood up and faced him. She made the "come and get me" motion with her hands. "Try me."

"No."

She reached to riffle his hair and Danya's hand circled her wrist, easing it away. His eyes were dark, his expression grim. "Don't. No wrestling."

Sidney eased down to sit beside him. She wasn't leaving him to brood about his lost love. They sat in silence, staring at the ocean, and she noted that he still held her hand, resting it on his thigh. Then suddenly, Danya said, "If you're ready, let's eat."

He'd locked himself inside again, she thought sadly. "Sure."

He held her hand on the way to his cabin, and waited until she opened the door for him to enter.

That gave her a chance to enjoy Danya's truly admirable backside. That warm little ball seemed to lodge low in Sidney's belly as she watched him; her throat dried and tightened and something had just peaked her breasts, though she wasn't cold. He was graceful, like a powerful cat, broad shoulders swaying just that bit, cords rippling down that T-shirt fitted so close to his body. She ached to take pictures of him, the blend of shadows and a truly sexy male.

He turned slowly and studied her with a half smile.

The hair on her nape lifted. She didn't understand that smile, but it caught her heart and flipped it over; her body quivered just that once, not in fear, but in anticipation—of what? Why was he looking at her like that—his lips curved slightly, his eyes heavy lidded, that silvery gaze taking in her body from head to foot? What was happening?

She wondered what it would feel like, nipple to nipple, hers to his, and her body went taut and hot and quivery again....

Danya slowly stripped away his T-shirt, his eyes never leaving hers. "I'll take another shower. Make yourself at home."

He didn't move. She couldn't move.

She could either call it a day and retreat.

Or she could— Sidney closed the cabin door behind her with a click.

Danya nodded slowly, then turned to go into the bathroom, leaving her alone.

Her knees shook; her whole body quivered. Whatever had happened in that moment had shaken her badly.

It was all in her mind, of course. Nothing had happened— not really.

Or had it?

Three

The poor guy was still in love with his wife and had not a clue that Sidney wanted to jump him. She really wanted to test that nipple to nipple idea.

Across the small table from her, Danya looked all shower-and-shampoo fresh and totally jumpable. His dark, shaggy hair was combed back from that hard, angular face, just reaching his shoulders. Candlelight emphasized the slant of his brows, the cut of his cheekbones, that sensual mouth.

That little quiver shot through Sidney again and she almost choked on the shrimp linguine he had expertly prepared. She lifted the wineglass and drank quickly.

"Okay?" Danya asked with concern.

He was such a nice guy, and she was thinking about that mouth and what it could do and what it would taste like—

Sidney reached for the bottle of wine and in passing, scorched her hand on the candle's flame— "Ouch!"

She started to rub it on her thigh, but Danya's hand took hers, his head bending.

His lips touched her hand, suckled the small wound slightly, and Sidney held her breath, fighting the sensations wrapping around her, tugging at her. "You can stop that. It doesn't hurt anymore," she whispered.

"Does it not?"

His voice was deep and intimate, with that bit of accent tugging at her—as if it were meant just for her. It hurt somewhere deep inside her, an unfamiliar sensitive part of her heart that she hadn't expected.

On the other hand—she wanted to jump him, take him, work up a real heated froth and exorcise that taut ache within her.

But then, she would be taking advantage of a sweet guy. Danya hadn't a clue, and he was still in love with his wife. Sidney watched him pour another glass of wine and noted that after he finished a sip, his lips were glossy and smooth.

She breathed deeply and quickly drank her wine. Danya leaned back in his chair. "Rough day?"

"I'm not a portrait photographer. It's tougher than I thought. I'm not used to arranging bodies and waiting for makeup and hair to be corrected. Earl, the makeup guy, got insulted when I asked him to help me with the light meter. The reason they wanted me for this gig was that I'm pretty good at natural settings and using natural light. Freelancing world catastrophes does a lot for picking up the pace and spotting good shots. Once, Ben and I were on the cusp of this volcano and the lava river swerved right toward us—"

"I see. How about having our wine out on the porch? It's relaxing to listen to the waves after a hard day."

On the porch step, Sidney sat beside Danya. "I never should have taken this job. I'll ship the takes to New York and they'll be processed there. I just didn't want to meet Ben and he doesn't do these gigs. It's more work than I expected—portraiture, I mean. Sometimes people freeze up and won't let the camera in. Even the models sometimes do that, and they're pros. I'll be glad when it's finished and I can see the finished product. Everything looks different once they do the graphic work and crop it."

Danya was holding her hand again, resting it on his thigh. He was silent, staring out into the ocean—probably missing his wife again.

He seemed so lonely and Sidney was glad that she was with him. "You've got to get out of this funk, guy," she said softly. "You'll meet someone and the first thing you know, you'll be adding cousins to the list already here."

"I would like children very much. Would you?"

"No. Rather, I never thought about it. Ben—"

"I would rather not hear about Ben, if that is okay with you."

"Oh, sure. I've been talking too much. It's boring, I know." Sidney yawned; she had began to feel the effects of the hard day, the good dinner and the wine.

"Tired?"

"Mmm. But I don't want to move. This is nice—the sound of the ocean, the tinkling of the wind chimes."

"Then rest here, against me." His arm came around her, easing her closer.

Just buddies in the night, Sidney thought, as she settled against him. "You'll get over this," she whispered.

"I don't think so," Danya returned unevenly as she slid into sleep with the ease of an experienced traveler, who took rest when possible.

Sidney awoke in Danya's big bed to the sound of deep strained breathing. Danya was on the floor, concentrating on push-ups. "It's still night, isn't it?" she asked drowsily as she eased to sit upright. "I usually do those in the morning."

"Morning is not far away. I am just getting a head start."

Sidney stood, yawned, stretched and shimmied out of her cargo pants. She tossed them over a chair and reached under her T-shirt, unfastening her bra and drawing it out one of her sleeves. She tossed it onto her pants and yawned again. "I'm beat."

Danya hadn't said anything, but in the shadows, his stare

was hard and narrowed upon her. He returned to his vigorous push-ups.

Sidney took in that long taut length, his bare back, those bulging muscles, that hard backside clad in jeans. "You ought to pace yourself, Danya."

"I am trying very hard to do just that."

"I don't remember getting into your bed, but I'll move to my sleeping bag. Thanks for letting me sleep a bit."

"Uh-huh," he said grimly.

Sidney walked into the bathroom and braced her hands against the closed door. Then she flattened herself against it and breathed hard, trying to understand what was happening to her. Danya, working up a sweat, had caused that quivery something inside her to tighten and hum and ache. She opted for a really cold shower, changed into her comfortable boxer shorts and T-shirt and came out into the room. Danya, probably exhausted, was lying stomach down on the floor, his head resting on his folded arms.

She thought about that nipple to nipple thing and tried to push it away—it wouldn't go.

Sidney lay down on her sleeping bag and covered up with her sheet. "Want to talk about it?"

He was lying very close on the floor beside her, and turned to stare at her. "With you? No."

"Why not?"

He jackknifed to his feet, stood over her and slowly took in the length of her body. The hard bulge beneath his jeans told her that he was aroused.

She could make use of that—if he didn't deserve better— some woman who would take good care of him.

On the other hand, waste not, want not—she thought as she stared up at him. "You're having a sexual moment, aren't you?"

"Isn't that obvious?"

"I've got no objections." It was the best invitation she could come up with and it had been good enough for Ben in close quarters.

Danya wasn't Ben—his smile wasn't nice, just a wolfish flash of teeth in the shadows. "But I do. We are friends, are we not?"

"Look, I know how it is with men. I was friends with Ben and we—"

"Just ships passing in the night, needs meeting needs, right?"

There was a taut, angry edge to his tone that caught her off guard, and caused her to feel guilty for some reason. She had the uneasy sense that if Danya wanted, he could be very dangerous. She wasn't certain that she liked "dangerous"; "comfortable" was much better. "It would be over in a minute. No strings attached. You'd sleep better."

"I would 'sleep better'? So you would sacrifice yourself? Your body to me and ask nothing, so that I would sleep better? Is that what you think lovemaking is between a man and a woman?" His head had tilted, his silvery blue eyes challenging her and that rigid jaw said that someone had crossed invisible male-female protocol lines.

Sidney thought of what she would be getting in return—quite a sizable commodity. "I'd be fine with that," she managed unevenly.

"I wouldn't be."

"Oh, your wife. I understand."

"I doubt it. You see, I need a little bit more than Ben apparently did."

Danya turned and walked into the bathroom and the shower began to run. When he emerged, he walked naked to the bed, and lay down with the sheet covering him, his back to Sidney. "Go to sleep, Sid."

Restless now, unsettled by the sight of Danya's naked body, it was a long time before Sidney could sleep.

He'd said "lovemaking," not "sex." *Lovemaking* had big connotations that Sidney did not want.

She had loved Ben, and she had been hurt.

Plain old sex served good enough in tight situations.

She tossed onto her stomach and fought the ache there and in her breasts. Sex was good enough, she repeated to herself. She'd leave "lovemaking" and "romance" to women who got soppy when they watched old movies and who wept at getting a bouquet of flowers. All those things were for people who had time for them; she didn't.

Sidney's restless turning, the muttering of Ben's name, had caused Danya to leave the cabin early. He walked down the beach and out onto the tourist pier where the row of shops was quiet and shadowy, the bright flags overhead flapping gently in the breeze. His father was sitting in a camping chair, a bucket of bait on the boards beside him. Dawn caught the thin silvery line stretched from Viktor Stepanov's pole into the huge dark waves.

"My son," Viktor said quietly. "I like this peaceful time. It reminds me of the old country, before my brothers and I leave. I am glad to be here with Fadey and my sons—my new granddaughter, Danika Louise. Someday, she will come fish with me, just as you and Alexi did as boys.... You want this woman, Sidney, for your own? I am glad. It is time. Sit. Talk with me."

"I want to marry her, Father. I want a home and children with her."

The Russian language flowed freely between Danya and his father now, the intimate quiet talk. "What is the problem then, my son?"

"She has not left the love she feels for another man. She moves quickly and will soon be gone."

"Then you will follow," Viktor stated with a shrug.

"Of course."

"Of course. But I think she fears what she feels for me. That it is confused with what she feels for this other man. I need time—"

"Give her what she needs. She will find you to be a good man and she will love only you, this I know. You bring her to your uncle Fadey's home, my home now. You let her meet us, see what we are. Pretty soon, you love, you marry, you have my grandchildren."

Danya smiled at his father's simple picture and looked at the gray sky foretelling morning and a clear day. The urge to make love to Sidney was strong, but he intended to move slowly, surely, into a relationship where she thought only of him—

Sidney had started working early, making use of wind and water to paste the model's swimsuits against their curves. The salt-scented ocean breeze lifted those masses of textured and colored hair up and away from beautiful, sculptured cheekbones. Earl was at his best, bronzing faces and long, bikini-clad bodies.

Sidney shot automatically, focusing on the best advantage of each face. Marvelous Calendars wanted every shot possible, for potential use in other sales promotions. They also wanted natural shots, the behind the scenes stuff for a potential documentary.

While Earl was working on Miss November, a blue-eyed sweet farm girl type from Wisconsin, Sidney swung her focus to Miss June. Alice Ann Michaels, in a worn flannel robe and huge black rimmed glasses, was absorbed in a thick book on law; Alice Ann was worried about passing the bar exams and she crammed every available moment.

Miss April sat in a beach chair, crocheting something big and maroon that she hauled from a tote bag at every available moment.

Miss February was skimming her notebook with one perfectly manicured fingernail, and talking earnestly on her cell phone. She was probably trading stocks and building her portfolio.

They were a good bunch, even if they were models and did obscene things to enhance their beauty, Sidney decided as she snapped away at the various models, waiting their turn at the camera. The models weren't so bad, really—if they didn't push to remake her into something she wasn't. Bulldog had never liked primpers.

Sidney directed Miss November's body draped over the light gray driftwood log. "Elbows back, face up, this way…just a little. Earl, get that strand of hair away from her face, and do something with that lip gloss—it's picking up too much sun…."

Because the day was warm and she was moving fast, leaping upon driftwood for better angles, crouching on the sand for upward shots, Sidney had skimmed down to her comfortable cutoff jean shorts and a sturdy black sports bra that allowed more freedom.

Sidney granted a long lunch break and rest for the models; they would begin calendar work again at three o'clock in the afternoon. Meanwhile, she placed a shirt over her sports bra and strolled around Amoteh, taking in the sights. She shot the colorful shops on the pier, the seagulls high in the clear blue sky, vacationers strolling hand in hand.

She spread a beach towel on the sand, leaned back and closed her eyes. She tried to picture Ben, a blond scholarly looking man, and instead Danya's rugged image came into her mind.

She thought she caught his scent, and smiled softly, then slowly opened her eyes to see Danya looking down at her. He was standing close and the wind had caught his hair, taking it back from those vivid blue eyes. "Hi," she whispered.

"Hi. Tired?"

"Mmm. Just relaxing. Sit down and pull up a piece of sand."

He sat beside her, staring out into the ocean, and Sidney studied him. "We were talking earlier about linking up—you know, men and women. What more do you need, Danya? I mean other than sex."

He watched a seagull darting among the strands of seaweed lying on the sand and took his time in answering. "I am old-fashioned. I need romance, I suppose."

"Kissing, foreplay, after play, et cetera. That kind of stuff?"

"Uh-huh."

"French kissing? Open lips, tongue on tongue, that sort of thing?"

He sounded strangled and cleared his throat. His gaze lowered to her chest and Sidney realized that she was too warm—probably because of the afternoon sun, magnified by the ocean waves—and her nipples had unexplainably hardened beneath the spandex confinement. "That would be acceptable," Danya agreed slowly.

"But all that would take a lot of time."

"That's true."

She had to have more answers. Ben had never wanted to talk about sex, and neither had Bulldog. In fact, Sidney's father got all flustered, huffy and reddish when his daughters pressed him. Danya seemed to have reliable information and wasn't averse to answering questions. "But—say one partner or the other got really aroused, and things went too fast and gee, there you were, all ready and nowhere to go?"

"I would take extreme care to see that my partner was—satisfied."

She patted his thigh. "I'm sure you would."

She wondered, while staring into Danya's very blue eyes, what would happen if her hand just happened to wander upward. She squeezed lightly, testing the solid pad of muscles beneath the denim.

"Don't," he ordered unevenly as his hand clamped over hers. "Don't even think about it. You're scaring me."

"Who me?" she asked and tried for a bland, innocent expression.

Danya inhaled abruptly, scowled at her, and stood. "I've got to get back to work."

Sidney came to her feet slowly. She didn't want him to go. She stood looking up at him, helpless with her emotions. Sidney wanted to run away from whatever was happening inside her—and she wanted Danya. Because she was uncertain, she hooked her thumbs into her cutoff shorts pockets.

She tingled and ached and couldn't look away from Danya's deep blue eyes. "I can't and won't take her place—your wife's place," she said unsteadily and wasn't certain what had caused that statement.

"You're nothing like her." The statement was soft and low and curled inside Sidney. Then Danya nodded to the woman coming toward them, an infant sleeping in the carrying sack in front of her. The woman's hair was black and sleek, tossed by the breeze. "This is my sister-in-law, Jessica, and that little beauty is Danika Louise."

Danya frowned at another woman with sun streaked hair walking toward them, carrying a baby. A young girl near her chased a giggling toddler. "That would be Ellie, Mikhail's wife with Tanya and Sasha."

He sucked in his breath and added, "The woman with all those curls is Leigh, Jarek's 'Precious', and she has my cousins, of course. They want to meet you. I had hoped to—"

"Oh, hi, Danya," Ellie said as she came to stand near them. "I didn't know you took work breaks in the middle of the day."

"Yes, I see that. Ah, here's my Sasha." He reached for the little girl who had come running and giggling into his arms. Danya made growling noises and nuzzled her throat while she squirmed and giggled happily.

When all of the women stood near, Danya introduced Sidney. "She likes to be called 'Sid.'"

"Oh, you're the photographer who's been taking pictures of the models," Jessica said. "We were wondering if you could take family pictures for all of us. If you have time— There isn't a photographer nearby and to get us all packed up and the children rested for a family portrait would be so much more difficult than having one taken here."

Danya cleared his throat and seemed uneasy. "She's not really a portrait photographer. This assignment is unusual for her. I'm sure she wouldn't have the time, anyway."

Ellie smiled sweetly. "But she just might want to, Danya."

He frowned at Ellie. "Of course. It is her decision."

Sidney stared at him; Danya didn't seem to want her to take

pictures of his family. "He's right. I'm learning. I usually do documentary type things, magazine spreads. This gig is new to me."

Danya lowered Sasha to the sand; he crossed his arms over his chest and looked forbidding as Ellie continued, "You must be good to be hired for calendar work. Mikhail may be asking you to do some shots for his new promotion brochure, and his mother is redoing the sales brochure for Stepanov Furniture."

"Ladies—" Danya began in what seemed might be a protest.

"And we thought maybe you could take pictures of us in Fadey's house, maybe do something for Fadey and Mary Lou's anniversary in late July," Leigh added. "Maybe something with Viktor and Alexi and Danya? Have you met Viktor, Danya's father? I think you should come to our afternoon tea and get a real feel for the family, and then you can decide."

Danya sighed as if outflanked and defeated. "I have to get back to work."

He looked at each woman and they smiled warmly back at him. Each one drew his head down for a kiss on the cheek. Danya shook his head and started back toward the house he was remodeling. Sidney noticed that two women lying on the beach were locked onto that tall, lean powerful male body striding away; she didn't like their lustful expressions one bit. She instantly decided not to even ask him if he wanted to model for her.

Sidney studied the Stepanov women, the different coloring, various heights and studied the babies held close to them. Together, they were beautiful and natural, and the contrast with the male counterparts would be exquisite.

Then, because Danya obviously didn't want her to work with them, she was intrigued, but she had to set the ground rules. She picked up her camera and began shooting the women and children's pictures, the wind tugging at their hair and clothes, a toddler sitting to sift sand through her fingers.

When she finished, she said, "I'll see that you get prints of these. I'm living with Danya, but don't get any ideas about romance in the mix. He's just offered me a place to rest. It gets hectic at the resort with all the models."

All three women agreed in a rush:

"Oh, Danya has made that perfectly clear."

"Crystal clear."

"He's already told us that you're just friends."

"I'll think about the family portraits and the brochures, but first I've got to finish this contract," Sidney said. "There's a big shindig at the resort tomorrow night, and I have to turn up—business, you know. But I've got to get something to wear. Is there a dress shop around here? I'll need something."

"Not really. It's mostly tourist stuff. I could maybe put something together for you—or alter it," Ellie said thoughtfully as she considered Sidney. "Come by the house when you get a break."

"She's a whiz with a sewing machine," Leigh said.

"Thanks. I may need to ask your help. I'm not much into clothes. I just need something that serves." In an elegant group, the models were moving down the steps of the Amoteh. "I have to get to work. Catch you later. Maybe. I'll get back to you about the portrait work."

As the women moved away, Sidney studied them. Clearly they were concerned for Danya.

When the shoot was over, Sidney took her daily takes up to the resort and expressed them to New York for processing. In the luxurious hallway, she met Mikhail. After a short conversation on the progress of the shoot, Mikhail said, "My wife has already told you that I would like you to do some promotion shots for the resort. I hope you're considering that. We need to update and my staff is comfortable with you."

"I'll think about it. Your family has already asked me to do portraits."

"We are overdue for that. We would so appreciate your attention."

"They're all so lovely. I'm considering it, but I don't usually stay long in one location. I'm a freelancer which means

I move around a lot. I've moved for most of my life—my dad was in the service."

"But you are more comfortable staying with Danya, than here at the resort?"

"The resort is really nice, very well run, Mikhail. But this particular gig has too many women in it and they're crowding me." After her exchange with the Stepanov women, Sidney's impression that Mikhail and all of his family hadn't cared about Danya had changed; she now saw that they were very concerned about him. "He's a great guy. I know he's mourning his wife. He'll find someone someday."

"Of course." With a brief smile Mikhail nodded and plucked the pager from his waist. He glanced at it. "I have to go. Some dilemma on the golf course. You are welcome in my home at any time."

Sidney decided to take more shots around Amoteh and wandered down to the docks. She took several of the tourist pier and children playing on the beach. She felt so much a part of everything she'd seen and done, and yet not a part of anything—as if she'd always been an observer, traveling on the perimeters of life.

She hadn't realized she was crying until she came to sit on the steps of Danya's cabin, surveying the evening's black rolling waves and thinking of the warmth and love of the Stepanov family. Sidney dashed away the tears and wrapped her arms around herself; the Stepanov women had their husbands and children and the images of the day skimmed through her mind. She had nothing in comparison.

Danya seemed to come out of the night, looming over her. "What's wrong?"

"Nothing. Everything."

He sat beside her and took her hand. He rubbed it between his warm ones. "What can I do?"

She wanted to be held and cuddled, but she was just having a silly feminine moment; she'd get over it soon enough. "I'm just down in the dumps. I get that way sometimes. It will go away. I'll be glad to get on the move again, get a new assignment somewhere else, life goes on, yada yada. I never cry, you know. I'm just getting all weirded out for some reason. Everything is off kilter here. Wrong, you know? I don't feel like myself. I mean, I think my work is really good or Jonesy says so—she's working on it in New York. But there's something else here, and it scares me."

"Ah. Maybe a change is good." His arm came around her, and Danya drew her close. She quivered again, the sensation that she was feminine and needed a man's strength was ridiculous, but still there. She moved into the sensation, testing it. She was definitely a great deal smaller than Danya, and probably less strong—but then she was very agile. So being smaller had advantages, too. She could probably be all over him in a minute—

"That's why you came here from Wyoming, isn't it? For the change?"

"It's been good for me."

Sidney looked up at Danya and studied him. She rarely touched anyone, unless it was to arrange them for a shoot, but just now—she found her fingertip moving over his face, taking in the sensations, the heat, the texture of his skin. He was new and yet familiar; he caused her to relax and to ache to have him. The contrast of all her emotions concerning him terrified her. "I'm scared, Danya. Really scared," she whispered.

"Of course. So am I." His kiss was light and friendly and with enough impact to stun her.

Sidney tried to catch her breath and suddenly she felt herself being lifted to sit on Danya's lap. "What's this? I'm not a kid and I'm not some overaged baby doll—"

"Shut up and stop squirming," he said pleasantly. "Has no one ever held you before? Like this? A man?"

"No one," she whispered back as she noted how Danya's hair felt in her fingers, the waves and the crisp texture.

"You can relax a little—against me."

It was a companionable thing to do, easing against Danya's hard body, testing the fit, the heat churning silently around them. "I don't know why I'm shaking," Sidney whispered.

"Neither do I."

"Shouldn't we be doing something? I mean we can't just sit here."

"Why not?"

"It's wasting time…." She wanted to stake him out and have him. But the poor guy was coping with enough problems. Sidney pushed away from Danya, stood, and rubbed her hands together. "So what's to eat? Shall we go out somewhere, pick up something?"

Danya's big hands settled on her hips and he drew her to stand between his knees. "Why are you so nervous, Sid?"

She couldn't say, *Gee, I'm having a sexual moment, Danya, and I want to nail you.*

Instead she said, "So you're going to be my date tomorrow night, right? Boy, I don't want to do the party thing. I usually just take off somewhere until the agony is over."

"Ah, that reminds me. Ellie said to get your measurements. She's already started on a dress—she's good at fittings and gauging from sight—but she wants you to stop by tomorrow afternoon for final adjustments. She sews for everyone and made me a shirt—she's made all the men in my family a shirt. Their women have embroidered them with old world designs—from some that my mother did for us as boys. Mine is as yet plain." He drew out a tape measure from his shirt pocket. "May I?"

Her body started doing that quaking thing—on the outside and the inside. "Sure," she managed. "Ellie can put a dress together just like that?"

"Mmm." Danya had slid the tape measure around Sidney's bust. He looked up at her. "Stand still. Stop fidgeting. Am I bothering you?"

His hands were resting over her breasts, bringing the ends of the tape measure together. In the moonlight, he leaned close to read the tape.

Sidney could have grabbed his head and pulled it close to her breasts—

Danya nodded and measured her waist, then her hips. He tucked the tape measure away and then fitted his hands around her waist, easing them up and under the loose shirt she wore. "Don't worry, Sidney," he whispered softly. "This will all work out."

"What are you talking about?"

"You're nervous of me."

She'd been through battlefields, avalanches, volcanoes, floods, earthquakes. She'd slept beside men in the African bush and on ship decks. "Hey, I work with men all the time—"

"But this is different, isn't it?"

But this is different, echoed in Sidney's mind as she tried to sleep later. *Very different.*

She was killing him, inch by inch, Danya decided early the next morning.

Restless and tossing on her sleeping bag, Sidney had talked in her sleep. Ben's name was noted frequently again. Danya intended to replace that name with his.

Sidney lay like a child, curled beneath the light sheet, her feet exposed. She had absolutely no idea of how attractive she was, how feminine.

How much of a curse she was to a man who had decided to take his time, building a solid relationship with her.

Danya answered the light rap on the door and with a sweep of his hand, invited Alexi into the cabin. "You brought them?"

Alexi took the small box from his shirt pocket and handed it to Danya, who indicated Sidney, sleeping on the floor. "I'm just fixing breakfast. Have some coffee?"

Alexi nodded and watched Sidney stir restlessly. He studied Danya in the way of one brother preparing to test another. "My wife says that if Sid needs a place to stay, she's welcome at our house."

"No." Danya cracked eggs into a bowl and added milk. He

whisked the mixture briskly before pouring it into a skillet sizzling with butter.

"Then Aunt Mary Jo and Uncle Fadey have plenty of room, even with our father staying there—"

"No." Danya eyed Alexi. "No, and double no."

"Oh. But look, she is sleeping on the floor. The least you could have done would have been to give her your bed."

"No."

Sidney yawned and turned to look at the men. "'Morning. Hi, Alexi."

She stood and stretched and started touching her toes. Her boxer shorts and Danya's overlarge T-shirt did little to hide her curves as she walked to the bathroom.

Alexi looked at Danya who was tracing the sway of her hips, his throat drying and every molecule in his body taut and aching.

"Your eggs are burning."

"Uh-huh. It is a nice day."

"It's snowing outside."

"Uh-huh."

"So she's the one, huh?"

This time, Danya turned to his brother. "She's driving me nuts. Not a clue."

Alexi started to chuckle and Danya scowled at him. Sidney chose that moment to walk out of the bathroom. She walked to the table, sat, placed her feet on the opposite chair and picked up a piece of toast, munching on it. "What's so funny?"

Danya carried the rest of the breakfast to the table and picked up her feet, placing them over his thigh as he sat. He held her ankles by gently resting his hand over them. When she tried to remove them, he shook his head. "The floor is cold in the morning. You aren't wearing socks.... And my brother has a strange sense of humor. He's just leaving."

Sidney dug into her eggs and toast, ran the back of her hand across her lips and sipped her coffee before speaking. "This is great."

When Alexi had gone, Sidney wiggled her toes against Danya's belly, just to see if whatever had passed between them last night was still simmering.

"Stop that," he ordered and lifted a piece of bacon to her lips. Sidney took a bite and decided to exchange the favor. She lifted another piece to his lips and wondered what he would do if she moved onto his lap...if she leaned against him as she had last night.

Danya's eyes darkened. "I don't know that I would like what you're thinking."

"About the dance?" she lied to divert him. "I was thinking that social hours and dances are a waste of time. I can't dance anyway. Never learned. I'm kind of a freestyle girl. I do really well at aborigine celebrations."

"Socializing and dancing are about getting to know each other. That takes time."

"I've never had a lot of time. Too busy."

"Make it."

"Why?"

With a brief smile that didn't reach his eyes, Danya released her ankles and stood, clearing away the table. "Ellie has your measurements. You're to stop at her home late this afternoon for a fitting. I'll meet you here and we'll go to the resort together."

"But I could meet you there."

"I will take you—that's how it works, Sidney. The man escorts the woman. You are the woman, and I am that man."

He seemed to be setting rules for her and that nettled. "Not if I have to be all coy and frilly."

Danya leveled a look at her. "Have I asked you to do that?"

"Just getting everything straight between us, guy. And by the way, I won't embarrass you by hanging all over you like some women do."

"If we go as a couple, there would have to be a certain amount of touching, don't you agree?"

"Just enough to get by, for looks," Sidney agreed and wondered how close and tight she could hold him to get a really good impression of that great body.

Four

"I can't wear these," Sidney said that evening as she looked at the delicate chandelier earrings resting in Danya's big callused palm. They were lovely, a circular shape shimmering with garnets and tiny fragile slices of gold dangling from them.

"They were my mother's. I would be honored."

"Well, that's just the point. These aren't cheap and what's more they are sentimental pieces. Your wife wore them, didn't she?"

"My wife preferred more modern jewelry."

Sidney ached to try the intricately fashioned earrings, just once, to see how she looked. Ellie's creation, a long, basic black gown moved sensuously along Sidney's body and she felt like a different person. "Oh. Still. I can't wear them. What if I would lose one?"

"You won't. It would please me, Sid."

"Well, okay. You're suffering enough, acting as my date. I feel exposed in this dress."

Danya bent to carefully insert the earrings into her ear

lobes, then leaned back to study the effect. His fingertip flicked one of the earrings and he grinned. "Beautiful."

He bent to give her a brief kiss that shocked her, then shrugged, dismissing the intimacy. "It is an occasion, is it not? You and I on a date? This is my first one in a long time."

"I...I've never had one. Sometimes Dad and Stretch and Junior and I go together."

"I hope I'll do."

Sidney was still dealing with that brief hard kiss when Danya ran his fingertip over the tiny shoulder straps and downward to trace the square tight bodice that lifted her breasts into curves. "You are lovely, Sid. Why fight it?"

"This is just so much of a waste of time and energy. I do good work. They've already said so. I don't know why I have to go through this agony."

Danya was staring down to her breasts and when his eyes lifted to meet hers, they were dark and primitive and shook something deep within her. "There's one more thing."

He walked to the refrigerator and removed a plastic box, placing it on the table.

Danya was beautiful, tall and in a white shirt, tie and a dark fitted suit; he could have been a male model posing for an exclusive clothing ad. He looked sleek and dangerous and experienced—very experienced and gorgeous.

As he walked toward her, the fragile orchid corsage in his hand, Sidney's heart started that strange flip-flopping again. She held her breath while he carefully bent to insert his fingers into her bodice and pinned the corsage. Because everything was too quiet and still—except within her shaking emotions—Sidney tried to speak. "I'm going to take your family's portraits—after this gig. I've got to do some stuff in New York to finalize, but I'll come back. It's the least I can do for this dress Ellie made. She's a whiz. She even borrowed a pair of shoes to match. I don't usually wear high heels—I hope I don't fall and embarrass you."

He seemed very intent upon fastening the corsage to the square cut of her gown. "Mmm."

"Shoes?" Sidney repeated, her mouth drying as his fingers slid inside her bodice to protect her from the corsage's pin. The pale orchid spotted with maroon drops was gorgeous. She'd press it and keep it and savor it after she had left Amoteh, just as she'd heard that other women did with flowers from special occasions. She had to have something to remember this night with Danya, even if it was a girly thing like a dead flattened flower. "They're going to be after you tonight. The models, I mean. Some of them are—well, man hungry like I told you, and on location they get—lonesome. I'll protect you, Danya. It's the least I can do for all this trouble."

"Thank you." He slowly removed his fingers and studied her. "What were you saying about shoes?"

"That Ellie borrowed just the right size to go with this dress. Look. I shaved my legs."

She extended one foot and the long gown's slit parted to show a bit of her leg. Danya crouched in front of her to study the black heels, his hand on her ankle. Then it slid slowly upward to rest briefly behind her thigh, drawing more of her leg into view. "They are nice and your leg is very smooth."

"Earl loaned me some makeup and he said to oil my legs so they shine and I wouldn't have to wear nylons. That would be real torture."

When Danya stood, his hands slid up over the gown, over her hips to her waist. "Shall we go?"

Sidney couldn't move, couldn't breathe and her heart raced wildly. "Okay. Let the pain begin."

A half hour later, Sidney held her shoes while Danya carried her from his truck in the parking lot into the Amoteh Resort. "I'm perfectly able to walk, Danya. You didn't have to carry me down your steps and all the way to your truck, or into the resort. What will people think? That I've sprained my ankle? Oh, boy, that's all I need—the models fussing over me...."

She felt light and feminine—and scared, and Danya wasn't making it any easier. He handled her easily, and just now he had just brushed a kiss against her temple. She just had to smooth those waves at his nape and stroke the smooth line of his jaw. In close proximity of a devastating male, preparing for an event, she'd been fascinated, watching him as he shaved in the bathroom with only a towel around his hips—until he closed the door in her face. She'd never done a nude male portrait, but she ached to "shoot" him. But to be truthful, she wanted to slide her hands over those powerful shoulders and back and chest and those hard little mounds of his butt and down to his thighs and in between and—

As Danya carried her toward the resort, he was looking at her breasts again, causing her unexplainable quiver. Sidney swallowed the tightness in her throat. "You smell great. Thank you for the corsage. It's my first."

Danya nodded grimly. He leveled a stare at the men waiting outside the resort's doorway—all the Stepanov males were standing there, grinning widely. An older man, slightly balding and shorter than the younger men, came forward. It was Viktor Stepanov whom she'd already met while hunting Danya. "My son," Viktor said formally.

"Father." Danya's acknowledgment was equally formal.

"I am honored," Viktor said as he took Sidney's hand and brought it to his lips. "You wear my wife's earrings well. That pleases me."

"They're beautiful. I'm not hurt or anything," Sidney felt obliged to say. "Danya just—"

Viktor smiled warmly. "My son wishes to carry you. I understand why."

"He's only being nice, but really, I can walk. Danya, put me down."

His answer was curt and adamant. "No."

"I could make you," she whispered in his ear.

"Could you?" His tone held a challenge.

Sidney watched the Stepanov wives come out of the resort and lean close against their husbands. She didn't understand what was happening, but suddenly she was amid the Stepanov family and Danya was holding her close. She tried to maintain appearances when she knew that her face was heating.

"Oh, hello, everyone," she managed lightly, and then the words just flew from her lips: "I'm not hurt. I can walk just fine. Isn't this corsage beautiful? It's my first. I didn't get Danya anything. Oh, no, I didn't get Danya anything, and look, he loaned me these beautiful earrings to go with this dress—Ellie made it in only a day, you know. She's wonderful, and yes, I would love to take your family portraits— Ah, this is a corsage, an orchid. No one else is wearing a corsage, Danya. Why am I?"

"Sid?" Danya whispered against her temple.

"Huh?"

"Hush. Everything will be just fine." He carried her into the resort and slowly placed her on her feet. Danya took the high strappy heels from her and kneeled to slide them onto her feet. He rose to turn her slowly until she faced a full length, massive mirror.

Sidney didn't recognize herself; standing in front of Danya, she looked sleek and beautiful, the earrings shimmering in her ears. She'd dabbed a bit of the model's makeup around her eyes and glossed her lips, and she looked feminine and—

"Beautiful," Danya whispered, his arms sliding around her from behind to draw her close to him.

She seemed so unfamiliar, this beautiful feminine woman, and terror spread through her. "This isn't me. I know it isn't. I want to go home, Danya. Let's leave now. Say I'm sick or something. And I really am getting that way," she added earnestly.

His opened lips moved against her nape, and then to her cheek leaving a heated trail as he whispered, "So you're running from a fight? You're afraid?"

Sidney looked over her shoulder to him. "You know that's not true. Why I've been in the middle of earthquakes, I've—"

His mind-blasting, devastating, gorgeous smile stopped her mind and she could just stare up at him. Danya took her hand and laced his fingers with hers. He felt solid and strong and good and a part of her. "We're still who we are, friends who met on Strawberry Hill, right? Let's go socialize, do our bit and then eat. I'm starving."

Who was she? Sidney wondered as they entered the Amoteh's ballroom and the Stepanov family came to surround them. Who was this beautiful woman, floating dreamily on a cloud?

She was going to do something wrong—she was going to embarrass Danya— "Let's leave now—"

Then she saw the models homing in on Danya, moving en masse toward them and she knew she had to protect him....

Danya looked down at the small woman standing protectively in front of him. "Back off," Sidney said firmly to the approaching tall svelte models. "You're not getting him. He's mine."

It wasn't exactly a declaration of love, but it would do, Danya thought with pleasure.

A tall sleek, raven-haired model and a blonde with a carefully tousled mane came close to study Sidney. "Sid?" The dark-haired woman asked tentatively.

"Sid?" the blonde asked, leaning down from her six-foot height to look at Sidney.

"Yeah. It's me. Just back off, will you? And if you make fun of me, just think of how I can make you look—really awful."

The models grinned impishly. "But, Sid, we wouldn't do that. We love you."

"Yeah, well, just don't try to cuddle me. I don't go in for that hugging, kissy-poo stuff. Back off, will you?"

A sultry redhead with green eyes came to stand near Danya. "You must be Mr. Wonderful. No wonder Sid has been keeping you under wraps."

"Misty, if you touch him, your takes are going to make you look like a hag," Sidney said quietly, dangerously.

Another model came to study Sidney and then all of them clustered around her. "My gosh, you're gorgeous, Sid."

Danya eased slightly away as the models surrounded Sidney. It was easy to see that they really cared for her, that their remarks were those of delight and discovery, not of jealousy.

"Look at those earrings. I've never seen you in earrings."

"Yeah, well, they're borrowed from Danya. They were his mother's. Just don't touch the flower."

"Oh, his mother's earrings and he gave you a corsage. Isn't that romantic, girls?"

Sidney looked up at Danya. "Romantic?" she whispered unevenly.

He recognized the stark fear in her expression, the widening of her eyes, the trembling of those soft lips. "We're friends," he stated as he reached to draw Sidney close to him.

"It's not a real date or anything, ladies. I just had to turn up and please the brass. He's doing me a favor."

"Then let me do my job." Danya drew her away from the women. He didn't want Sidney frightened of a situation that might implicate a long-term commitment.

Sidney introduced him to a realm of executives who seemed even more fascinated with her appearance.

"Dance later?" one of the men asked as his gaze took in Sidney's curved body.

"We've danced before, Ed. You didn't like it," she said.

"Things are looking quite different now, Sid. I'll like it."

Danya held his breath. Every decision Sidney made had to be hers. He relaxed slightly when Sidney eased back against him. Over her head, he leveled a cold meaningful stare at Ed. The other man frowned slightly, then nodded as if he understood.

As Sidney and Danya danced later, he met Alexi's stare; the Stepanov family recognized his claiming of Sidney. Now all Danya had to do was to make certain that she understood that she was already a part of his heart, that already she was his wife, without frightening her.

Then there was the matter of Ben. Danya didn't want Sidney on the rebound, still loving Ben.

Danya's patience in handling Sidney hadn't been easy;

earlier while he'd shaved and she'd come to study him, he'd recognized the desire in those beautiful large brown eyes; he'd felt her body quiver, the call of it starkly answered by his own taut one. The towel around his hips had been slightly damp and had revealed his bold erection.

His brief experience with Sidney had been very painful, but he could wait.

She had to know her own mind and he could be very patient.

While they danced, Danya forced himself to follow Sidney's abrupt push and shove lead. It didn't really matter to him, so long as her arms were around him, her body tight against his.

"You're awfully big and hard to move around," she whispered.

"Let's try something different—put your arms around my neck and just rest a while."

"But that would squash my flower, wouldn't it?"

"We'll be careful."

"Maybe this isn't such a good idea," Sidney whispered as she rested close to Danya.

In the privacy of a shadowy corner, they swayed to the music. Those dark brown eyes studied him for a moment and then Sidney stood on tiptoe, reached for his head and tugged him down to her.

Her kiss was open and hot and he sank into it, his hands open on her body, dragging her close to him. The sounds that came from deep inside her throat were those of a woman aching for fulfillment, her body pressing, moving against his.

In the shadows of the dance floor, the heat rose too quickly between them. "Sidney—"

Her hands ran inside his jacket, up over his back, her breath coming in short pants against his cheek.

Sidney was explosively aroused, the heat pouring from her and Danya had to move fast. "Let's go."

He intended to take her someplace quiet, where he could soothe and cool the throbbing heat between them. He feared for her embarrassment, for any repercussions from her business associates, and he needed to take her to safety.

Inside the display room for Stepanov Furniture, Danya locked the door behind them. "Sidney—"

She pressed close to him, backing him against the door, her lips open against his, her tongue flicking, sucking, her hips moving against him. "Danya...."

The sound of his name, the feminine ache curling around it, the heat of her body, the incredible scent of her arousal sent him over the edge. He had to be in her, with her, moving, flowing, taking....

Sidney had pushed away momentarily, and in the shadowy display room, her body was outlined in front of the massive windows as she quickly eased the dress down and away. She was nude and pale and—

"You're not wearing anything under that?" he asked in a strangled voice, because if he had known earlier—

"Bare skin. The models said that panty lines ruin the effect and I don't have any of their thong type. Am I okay?"

Her body was perfect, all curves and softness and fragrant smooth skin. He traced the roundness of her breasts, the darkness of her nipples, the curve of her body into that tiny waist, the flare of her hips, the dark triangle between her thighs.

Then all the blood in his body had seemed to boil and to lodge low in his body. He had to have just a taste, no more, Danya promised himself as he tugged her close to him.

He had to taste her, to feel her body move against his, to cup her breasts. Once his lips were on her breasts, Sidney seemed to explode in a heated storm....

Suddenly her hands were tearing at his jacket, his shirt and tie, and his belt. Once her hand touched him through his slacks, enfolded him, Danya shook, fighting his desire. "I want to wait," he managed unevenly even as his hand skimmed over her body.

"For what? Why not now? Oh, right there, touch me there," Sidney whispered as his fingers found dampness and heat.

"Say my name." He had to know that she wanted only him.

"Danya…." came in a soft quiet cry that tossed away all doubt—

Sidney watched Danya strip away the rest of his clothing and pull back the coverlet and the top black satin sheet. He was hot and taut and shaking and perfect as he lowered her to the cool sheet. His primitive expression told her that he wanted her; his hands flowing over her, heating her.

She moved against him, desperate for him, but she was frightened, too…because Danya was too intense, his hands firm and possessive, his eyes slitted as he looked down the length of her body. He touched and caressed her body as if he were claiming her forever, making her a part of him, of his life that would never change. He bent over her, kissed her lightly, sweetly, and nuzzled her cheek with his own. "Who am I?" he asked huskily again. "Say my name."

Sidney trembled in anticipation and in fear and ached for him to take her. His lips prowled her ears, her temples, her cheeks and returned to her lips. Against them, he asked again, "Who am I?"

She'd had sex with Ben, welcomed the brief joining, the light but unsatisfying bliss that followed. But Danya was taking his time, and he wanted more—he wanted possession; he wanted everything and she knew she'd never forget him, that the imprint of his lips, his hands, the taste of his lips would stay with her forever.

But then, she didn't want him to forget her, either. "You first. Say my name."

"You're the only woman in my arms now."

"I can't be someone else," she whispered unevenly; she wouldn't substitute for his wife.

His tone held arrogance and pleasure: "Of course, Sidney."

She couldn't resist touching his face, smoothing the hard lines, that sharp ridge of his cheekbone, his hard jaw, those sensuous lips that kissed her fingertips. "This is taking a lot of time, Danya."

"It is good, is it not?" he asked as his head descended to rest upon her breasts, to tempt them with soft open kisses.

"I can't think now," she managed as his lips moved upon her nipples, tongue and teeth tormenting them. She dug her fingers into his shoulders. "But you're not going anywhere."

His smile curved upon her stomach and Sidney sucked in her breath. "You're getting a little familiar there, partner."

Danya eased back up her body and reached for his slacks; she recognized the brief movement in which he prepared himself before moving over her, bracing his weight away. He looked down to where her breasts met his chest, and moved sensuously against her. "You're very small, Sidney. I'm afraid to hurt you."

She trembled at the thought of his body entering hers and yet she had to have him, claim him. Arching against Danya, Sidney eased her legs around his, rocking slightly, reaching up to tug his head down to hers. His lips parted upon hers, slanted and fastened until his taste was hers, his breath was hers. "Slowly, Sidney, slowly—" he whispered as she began to tremble, needing him.

The first blunt touch of him caused her to tense, her body reacting tautly to sharing with him even as she ached for completion.

The words he murmured against her ear, soft and low and sweet, were foreign but they curled around her, calmed her as Danya slowly entered her body. "Danya...Danya... Danya...."

They moved together, dreamily, kisses sweet and tender, and then suddenly, she tumbled into a frenzy, drawing him deep and tight, and Danya moved heavier, more forcefully in their fierce, hot battle as she pitted herself against him, the building pressure within herself.

Pulsating with fever, Sidney forgot everything but the fire between them, the claiming of Danya.

The ultimate pleasure seemed to last forever, holding her at the tip, and Danya stilled— "Look at me," he demanded fiercely.

Inside herself now, fighting herself and the pleasure, Sidney forced her eyes open to Danya's primitive expression. "Danya—" she whispered as once again pleasure exploded within her.

She floated downward, held securely in his arms and nestled against him; her arms and legs holding him close.

The soft kisses and gentle caresses brought her slowly to the surface, to the scent of him beside her, to the slowing rhythm of his heart. Danya eased the black satin sheet over them and held her closer, as if she were a part of him.

Sidney hadn't indulged in tasting a man, but now, she had to taste Danya's muscular throat, to feel his pulse run hot and wild beneath her lips. Still caught by the wonder of what had passed between them—soft and gentle, then hot and wild— she ran her hand over his chest, enjoying the feel of his big body in her arms. "You used protection."

"Of course. You move fast in everything you do. I wanted to be prepared."

"People might wonder about us."

"Let them wonder. The door is locked…the Do Not Enter sign is on it."

"I want to go." She was afraid now, afraid that Danya's lovemaking meant too much, that now she was a part of him— and that would only mean pain later on. She wasn't meant to be a wife, such as she'd seen in the Stepanov women. She wasn't meant to stay in one place, become an integral part of a family— "I don't like this."

His hands tightened on her for a moment, then Danya jack-knifed into sitting, his broad back to her. "Okay. Fine. Let's go."

She sensed that she had hurt him somehow, but overwhelmed with his lovemaking, her body aching slightly, she had to reclaim herself.

Danya turned suddenly and placed his open hand flat over her stomach. "Are you okay?"

"You talk too much," she whispered as she eased away. "We're done now, you know."

"Are we? You think we're done now?…. Ah, of course. You're nervous of this new phase."

"That wasn't sex, Danya. You were doing something else, taking all that time and—you were so into it."

He lifted a thick eyebrow. "And you weren't?"

"I want to go home. Everything is just too much. Now, Danya, please, before someone sees—"

"Sees how I have marked you—how flushed and dazed you look, how soft? As if you've just made love?"

Sidney lowered her head; she had never blushed and now her face was hot. Danya's fingertip lifted her chin, his kiss light upon her lips. "Okay, let's go."

Five

Sidney lay on her sleeping bag in Danya's cabin, her mind too busy for sleep. Outside, the wind chimes tinkled softly, churned by the Pacific's light breeze.

None of what had happened hours before was real—not the dress, the earrings, or the woman she'd been for a few hours.

But Danya's lovemaking was definitely real, her body aching slightly, her breasts sensitized as she flopped to her stomach and punched her pillow. She could almost feel the glide of the black satin sheet beneath her, the hard rhythm of Danya's body meeting hers, the heat of him, that last pulsating feverish moment when everything stopped.

The distance of twenty feet stretched between her sleeping bag and his bed, and the man lying upon it—still and awake.

She could still feel him in her, feel the taste of his lips— He'd made love to her, taking his time gently.

As he had when leaving the cabin, Danya had carried her up the steps and into it, placing her gently upon her feet.

"Scared?" he'd asked gently when she'd placed the earrings into his hand, returning the mark of his possession, a physical notation that she belonged to him.

"I don't want to talk now. This whole night isn't real."

"But it is."

She hadn't wanted to look up at him, to feel feminine and soft and small. Those emotions were unfamiliar and terrifying. "I had the feeling that you were—that you were doing something else than sex—I mean more than the physical, which was pretty good, by the way."

His "Thanks" had seemed to be wrapped in humor. Danya's fingertip had run around her ear. "What did you think was happening—other than the obvious?"

"It was weird." Those were comfortable, but inappropriate words. Lovemaking with Danya had seemed magical, overwhelming, gentle, fierce, passionate.

She'd never seen herself as a passionate woman—except as passionate about her work, the details, the composition of light and shadow. Yet she'd demanded as much from Danya as he had from her.

At his touch, she had trembled, and knew that her body recognized his, wanting more, and she'd walked into the bathroom to give herself space, to recover from whatever was happening to her. In the bald light, her reflection in the mirror had been stark—her face pale, eyes huge and dark and mysterious, and her lips had been soft and swollen, the face of a woman who had been thoroughly loved. In their passion, she'd cried out his name, and then the other sounds so unlike her, deep in her throat, primitive noises. The tears she'd held spilled down her cheeks and she didn't know why.

Those tears were still inside her, the uncertainty of who she was, the fear of what had happened—no light passing sexual encounter, but a deep primitive bonding.

Who was she? Was she tough, capable Sid Blakely who never stayed in one place longer than her work demanded? Who never failed at anything she wanted to do? Or was she this other woman, who cried and ached to be held? Who was this woman who hadn't just had quick sex, but who had made fierce, shocking love to a man? Who had returned his touch, just as hungrily, who had met that fiery heat, demanding her own fulfillment?

Sidney turned to look at Danya, lying on his bed. In the shadows, his eyes were slits of silver, watching her.

She felt herself in motion, following the call of his body and the need to be close to him, and then she was standing beside his bed.

Danya simply lifted his hand, and, taking it, she slid in beside him, into his arms. Nestled against him and exhausted by her emotions, Sidney listened to the slow strong beat of his heart and gave herself to sleep.

Danya lay still, feeling Sidney ease from him.

He'd been awake through the night, cherishing her body close to his, wondering how she would react in the morning. He could only wait for Sidney to work through her conflicts, but it wouldn't be easy for him, not after he'd tasted her body, felt it tremble and accept his own. He'd planned for a growing relationship, but Sidney's response had swept them into a passionate storm.

In the morning shadows, Sidney dressed quickly, rolled her sleeping bag, and then paused to smooth her gown which rested upon the back of a chair. She ran her fingertip over the earrings left on the table, and then she walked back to stand beside him.

Danya pretended to be asleep as her fingers traveled lightly over his face, and forced himself not to return the light kiss she gave him.

Sidney slid silently from the cabin and Danya watched the door close before he was on his feet. He couldn't let her leave without something to remind her of him. He grabbed the earrings, jerked open the door and went down the steps, catching her on the beach. "Sidney, you forgot something."

In the light of dawn, she stared down at the earrings in his hand. "I can't take those."

"Please."

"You're standing naked on the beach, you know. Someone will notice."

Then her gaze took him in, all of him, and she quivered slightly. "Cold?" he asked gently, when he knew what she wanted—the same as he.

"You're not going inside until I take those earrings, are you?"

He smiled at that and shook his head. "See? You know me so well already. I have no mystery left."

"Well, right now, with you naked and…" Her eyes had lowered, tracing his body and in the pink tinge rising up her cheeks wasn't from the dawn.

Once he folded the earrings into her hand, Danya brought her fingers to his lips. "Here's something you forgot."

With that, he tugged her into his arms and kissed her with all the passion brewing in him—anger, fear for her, for himself and the love he already felt, tenderness and a deep need to bond with her on that primitive level again….

Because he feared his stark emotions, Danya thrust her away and turned to walk back to the cabin.

He left her standing dazed upon the sandy beach, his earrings in her hand and his kiss upon her lips.

Either she'd remember him or not, he decided grimly as he rubbed the ache in his chest, his heart. Either she would come back, or she wouldn't.

The decision was hers.

In the small New York City studio apartment she had leased for a home base, Sidney pulled a candy bar from her cargo pants and watched streaks of June rain slide down the window. The candle she'd placed in an unused ashtray flickered slightly, casting shadows upon the barren walls. It was the first candle Sidney had purchased in her lifetime—because it reminded her of the dinner Danya had cooked for her.

Now that was truly strange, she reflected, that a man would cook for her. Correction: that he would cook expressly for her.

In the three days that Sidney had been in New York, she'd wrapped up her job with Marvelous Calendar Company. Jonesy had been pleased with her work and the photos were being cropped and processed for the calendar. Marvelous Calendar had given her a nice bonus. Several offers had come through via e-mail, but she hadn't accepted them. She'd created a nice little sturdy professional niche and word had gotten around that she was reliable good quality. That equated to jobs. Career-wise, things couldn't be better.

The models had sent the customary thank-yous with a twist this time: they were friendly and warm, adding tidbits about their private lives, inviting her to their homes, and adding that they wanted to be put on her wedding invitation list. Somehow, they'd gotten the wrong impression; marriage wasn't on Sidney's to-do list.

The let's-be-friends-for-Ben's sake/come-see-us letter that Fluffy had written was among the stack of mail on the coffee table. "Yeah, right, Fluffy."

The ache to see Ben was there, her longtime friend with whom she had shared so much of her career. Pregnant now, Fluffy wanted Sidney to be a godmother to their child.

"No thanks, Fluffy." Sidney looked out at the night and the rain. She had never thought of herself as a wife, or as a mother and she couldn't explain the ache that Fluffy's news had begun.

Was a career all she had? Sidney asked herself as she munched on a chocolate bar. There was Bulldog, Stretch and Junior, of course, and they connected by e-mail, telephone and came together at times when convenient or when various dangers happened to each other.

Stretch and Junior had already called, somehow sensing Sidney's uneasiness. Their questions were sly, well-packaged but underlined with concern for her. How could she tell them that she felt as if her whole world was coming apart? That little pieces of her were uncertain?

The telephone rang and when the message machine started

to record Bulldog's gruff, clipped tones, Sidney picked up. "Hi, Bulldog."

In typical fashion, he wasted no time in getting to the reason he had called. "Stretch and Junior are worried about you. What's up? If it's that damn Ben again, I'll take care of him pronto."

Her father could be irritating and his manners were abrupt, but he cared deeply about her. Sidney took another bite of her chocolate bar and the other end of the line seemed to explode: "What's that I hear? Candy-bar paper? You know that stuff isn't healthy and you've got to be careful of what you eat. Now, I know you're upset. Your mother always did the same thing—made a beeline for chocolate the minute she got upset. And you're upset, aren't you? You're not crying, are you?" her father demanded. "A Blakely never cries, Sid."

Sidney swallowed the bite of candy and wiped a tear from the corner of her eye; for some reason, she felt weepy and soft as a sponge filled with water. Bulldog proceeded to pinpoint her problem. "I don't like this candy bar business and I want to get to the bottom of this now…. Okay, your last assignment was for a calendar. What the hell are you doing wasting your talent on some light-brained job like that? You ought to be out in the middle of some earthquake, a forest fire or something."

"The pay is good, Bulldog. The ground is steady beneath my feet for good shots and I'm not having to raise my camera up high while wading through a swamp filled with alligators. Not a leech in sight."

"Yeah, well," he grumbled. "Something sure as hell is wrong with you. Did you just sniff? Dammit, Sid, crying never solves anything. It's action that counts—"

She'd had action—of the lovemaking kind with Danya, slow, thorough, fierce…

"It's the fourth week of June, you know. And I have a summer cold," she lied. When aroused, fearing for her, Bulldog, Stretch and Junior would all rush to her rescue. She'd had to play down her disappointment with Ben to stop Bulldog from entering a full-out war. "I'm having a cough drop. That was the paper you heard rattling."

That pacified Bulldog momentarily. Then he said, "Stretch and Junior say you aren't yourself. Either you tell me, or I'm flying to New York—wait a minute, if you had trouble, it might have been in that town on the Pacific. Amoteh, wasn't it? It won't take long to fly from here in Maine over there and—"

That terrified her. Everyone in Amoteh knew she had stayed with Danya for a few days, that she'd dressed in a gown, and had danced with him. Bulldog would be on Danya within minutes of landing in Amoteh.

She stroked the delicate earring in her ear. Louise Stepanov's beautiful earrings were delicate and feminine and didn't match Sidney's T-shirt, cargo pants and boots, but she couldn't bear to take them off. She only wore them when she was inside the apartment though, fearing she would lose one.

Why would Danya want her to take something so precious to his family, earrings that had belonged to his mother? "I would be honored," he'd said.

Sidney flipped to the orchid corsage she'd pressed, remembering how intent Danya had been as he fastened it to her gown.... She had to stop her father from confronting Danya. The only way to take a firm stand against Bulldog was to hit him between the eyes with good solid truth, or else he'd take over "Look, Bulldog, I know you care. But you mess in my life right now, and I won't be happy. I'm feeling pretty bad because I failed with Ben, and I'm working things out."

On the other end of the line, her father sputtered and cleared his throat. "Half pint, that is no way to speak to your old man."

"Just making my orders clear, sir."

"Good enough. Call me if you need backup."

Because he was her father and she loved him, Sidney asked a question that had been bothering her since Fluffy's pregnancy-announcement/godmother-request letter: "So, Bulldog, have you ever wanted to be a grandfather?"

The silence at the other end of the line told Sidney that her father was stunned and trying to recover. "Are you pregnant, Sid?" he asked cautiously. "How the hell did that happen?"

"I'm not, but I guess it might happen the usual way—if I were, that is. I'm a woman, you know."

"Oh, damn. You always were fast on the move. You don't have one of those devilish, female biological urges do you? Now, Sid, think twice. You weren't cut out for wife and mother duty."

"That's not in my life plan at all. You know I love traveling and my work. It's exciting and I'm good at it—and by the way, Bulldog, your wife was mother material."

"Sara was…special. I just wish she could have lived long enough to see you all doing so well." Bulldog's voice had softened. "But you girls were always more like me—on the move, busy with your careers, in the middle of everything. Sure, Sara had moods sometimes that I didn't understand, and so do you girls, but you know you can count on me, Sid."

"I'm just going through some things, Dad. I'm fine," Sidney stated carefully.

"When you call me 'Dad,' I know it's serious. Keep me posted, or I'll break that cease-and-desist order," her father ordered before abruptly ending the call.

Sidney finished her candy bar and reached into her cargo pocket for another. With Ben settled in a farm in Wisconsin, raising ducks and immersing himself in fatherhood and Fluffy, she wouldn't have to worry about meeting him in some jungle camp where the inevitable was—inevitable. She hadn't told him off yet, and she just had to finish that job. In close proximity, she was certain to attack him, verbally, and just maybe toss him a few times. The thought that Fluffy and Ben wanted her as a godmother for their baby caused her to frown. "When hell freezes over, chum."

She crossed her boots that were resting on the arm of the couch and considered her next move…. Any number of assignments waited for her, but memories of Danya kept interfering with clear thinking. On impulse, she unlaced her boots, stripped off her socks and wiggled her toes, still painted with dark red polish.

The unfamiliar sensual moment drew her thoughts to Ben. Compared to Danya, Ben had never seemed primitive during sex—or as thorough. Mr. Rabbit was only concerned about one thing; Danya seemed to have other motives and definitely had been a very thorough lover.

But then, they'd met on a very high cliff doing the midnight moody thing, and missing his wife, he was getting ready to end it all.

Transference was a potent motivator, and she just might have been the object Danya had transferred to—if so, he did it very well. Picking through the logical pieces of what had happened between them was easy, and on a whim, Sidney decided to call Danya. Uncertain how to best reach him, she left a message on the Stepanov Building Company machine, then settled back to mentally script her talk with him—if he returned the call.

She'd promised to take the Stepanov family pictures, and there would be no way to do that without interacting with Danya.

Well, okay. If she went back to Amoteh, and Danya seemed okay with it, they could have very satisfying, earthshaking sex.

That is, if he hadn't made complete emotional transference from missing his wife to Sidney.

On impulse, Sidney stood up and walked into a bedroom she seldom used for anything other than storage of her work. She tugged off her clothing and considered herself in the full-length mirror.

Danya's earrings caught the light, sparkling in her reflection. She'd been right, when howling at the moon on Strawberry Hill and talking with the chieftain entombed there: She did have all the basic equipment, which was now sensitized and aching and lonely. She glanced at her bed, heaped with boxes of her work.

If she had Danya on that bed right now, she'd—

The telephone rang and Sidney waited until Danya's deep voice came into the room. "I miss you," he said simply and the line clicked off.

Sidney quickly redialed the Stepanov Building number and Danya answered. "Hi," she managed breathlessly.

"Hi."

"Sex with you wasn't so bad," she said, surprising herself and knew instantly that Danya had the power to bring things to her mind and lips that would never have previously escaped.

There was a long pause before Danya murmured dryly, "Thanks. You weren't so bad either."

Now that was real encouragement, coming from a romantic sort of guy. "I'm wearing your earrings…um, just thought you'd want to know. I'm taking really good care of them."

Danya cleared his throat, his tone uneven as he asked, "Anything else? Are you wearing anything else?"

He was the first man to be interested in what she was wearing. Sidney held her breath as she answered, "Not a thing. Nope. Just those earrings."

Then it seemed appropriate to ask, "So what are you wearing, guy?"

"Skin."

Sidney thought of Danya's smooth skin covering all those powerful muscles and deep within her that clenching ache began. She turned to the full-length mirror and remembered when Danya had stood behind her at the Amoteh Resort, his open hands pressing her close. The image was sensual and standing without clothing, she could easily remember Danya's hard body against hers. "Oh."

"Your skin is very soft. I love to taste it—all over."

She forced a swallow down her dry, tight throat. "Oh."

Tit for tat, she thought and searched for equal footing in whatever was going on between them. She wanted to be held tight against him, to lock him to her, flying through pleasure and heartbeats and that passionate storm at the end. "Your butt is cute."

"Thanks. So is yours."

"I'm overweight now. Fat grabs on to my butt and my chest."

"You're perfect, Sidney…curvy and feminine. If you were here right now, I'd be in you, making love to you. I'd be waiting for those sounds you make, like purring and then like hunger."

That shocked her, that a man would speak so openly. "Hey, what?"

"In you, making love," he repeated slowly, softly, and Sidney's heartbeat kicked up, her body started trembling. "I'd cherish that little scream at the end. But the next time, don't bother to try to hold it in."

"Now that is just plain offensive. You're saying I'm noisy."

Danya chuckled on the other end of the line. "Sweetheart, I'm saying I like it. Good night."

After the call ended, Sidney debated the word "sweetheart," as applied to her specifically. "The guy is a real romantic and he's lonesome. I saved him from jumping—though he's not admitting it—and he's got a little transference thing from his wife going on. He'll get over it."

But would she?

Would she ever be able to forget Danya?

Sidney placed the telephone on a stack of brochures for the Cayman Islands. She'd taken the pictures, done the scuba diving shots, and had picked up a nice little fee. Taking photos of the Amoteh Resort wouldn't take long, and taking pictures of the Stepanov family would let her experiment with portraits of children and those faces with a few lines of experience, like Fadey and Viktor. It would be all light and shadow and beaches and sky and—and Danya.

Sidney decided that what had happened with Danya wasn't finished and taking those jobs would be the perfect time to see more of him—on a friendly basis. Nothing permanent, of course. Because eventually he'd find someone who matched the wife and children and home picture he should have. Everything was about pictures when you really came down to it, she decided. Some compositions fit and others just didn't.

She'd seen him over one rough spot, after all, she justified, and she couldn't just desert him.

On the other hand, she couldn't use him as a toy boy, either.

Not that Danya was a boy, of course; he was very much a full grown and very hot male. And not her type.

With a sigh, Sidney took a folded sheet from her linen closet, wrapped it around her and went to lie on her couch. She'd be worthless on a photo shoot if she couldn't focus and that was her problem right now.

She needed to complete her Danya-assignment, needed closure to her uneasiness, and then life would move on as it had.

Sidney removed an earring and lifted it to the light, studying it. Glittering in the shadows, it represented Danya and too many unseen dangers. She couldn't be what he needed; Ben had made it quite clear that she wasn't appealing as a wife. "You're okay, Sid," Ben had said. "But I love Fluffy. You understand why a man would want a woman like her, want to settle down, right? Thanks, Sid, I knew you'd understand. You've always been a good buddy."

She didn't want to be Danya's "good buddy," and she didn't want to hurt him either.

She reached for the telephone and dialed his number. Someone picked up, and Sidney's heart beat quickly as she waited for Danya's voice. "Sidney?"

All of her fears and thoughts came rushing out. "I'll get someone to do your family portraits. Someone really good, who specializes in that—I don't. I just took the gig at Amoteh because I didn't want to run into Ben, but now I don't have to worry about that as he's not leaving Fluffy—she's pregnant, you know. They're raising ducks in Wisconsin. I like duck *a l'orange,* but I wouldn't want to murder one to feed myself. I'll send the earrings and insure them. They belong to your family and I don't know why you would give them to me, or why I would take them. We had sex. It was good. I don't need payoff for that. Consider the account closed. You're okay now and you don't owe me anything. I don't want to be your sometimes-on and sometimes-off. You should marry someone and have that family. I'm not coming back. Bye."

She waited for Danya to end the conversation and the silence at the other end of the line stretched with her every heartbeat. Finally, Danya spoke and every word was wrapped in cold, tight anger. "Okay, Sidney...if that's the way you want it. But I never thought you were a quitter or a coward. Goodbye."

"Listen, guy. I am not a quitter or a coward—" She looked at the telephone which had just clicked and was buzzing with an empty sound. She redialed, because Danya wasn't getting the last word. The telephone rang several times before she hung up. "I am not a quitter, Mr. Danya Stepanov. I just think someone else would do a better job of the portraits, that's all."

But that wasn't the issue, and Sidney knew it. Something wove between Danya and herself, and it terrified her.

She should run, not walk to the nearest exit.

But could she?

Six

Danya concentrated on hand-sanding the small feminine vanity. In dark walnut and soon to be fitted with an oval mirror, it would be perfect for Sidney. He could almost see her sitting at it, dainty hands brushing her hair. The stool was already finished, a small plain design that would require a cushioned pad. The furniture gave him something to do while brooding about Sidney; he was torn between going after her and trying a friendly, romantic approach, and telling her just how irritating she was....

On the first of July, it had been just over two weeks since he'd first met her on Strawberry Hill; he was beginning to wonder if Chief Kamakani's curse on Amoteh wasn't a legend, but that truth was wrapped in one irritating woman who thought Danya had given her those earrings as payment for sex.

At five o'clock, the Stepanov Furniture Shop was filled with blaring Russian folk music and the sound of various sanders and saws. His brother, Alexi, his cousins, Mikhail and

Jarek, his uncle Fadey and father Viktor had all met in the shop earlier. Periodically Fadey and Viktor yelled "Hey!," hooked arms and with their free arms held high, danced around each other. Perhaps it was only because they were worried about him and had come to keep him company, because they understood that he was brooding about his love—*Danya's irritating, stubborn, take charge, terrified woman who actually thought he would gift her with his mother's earrings as payment for sex.*

But then Sidney was still brooding about Ben, and certain that Danya was looking for a woman like his deceased love.

If he had Sidney in his hands, he'd make certain she knew that she belonged to him. Danya inhaled deeply; he wasn't an impatient man, or a possessive one, but Sidney had changed him. He smoothed the walnut surface and tested the slide of the drawers on either side of the knee hole— Sidney had beautiful knees, strong thighs, and little feet that pressed down when she—

He closed the drawer too suddenly and Alexi came to stand beside him. He handed Danya a raspberry-filled cookie. "It's been over a week since you spoke to her on the telephone. You could make the first move."

"I could."

"Killing you not to, right?" Alexi asked knowingly.

"She's frustrating and irritating and yes, it is killing me not to call her again."

"That's saying a lot—you're hard to irritate and as your older brother, who's done a lot of tormenting you, I should know." Alexi considered the small vanity. "Good lines. Sturdy, not too feminine. You'll have to be careful of the drawer pulls, not too ornate. She'll like that. Any woman would."

Danya met his brother's eyes, as blue as his own. "Sidney isn't any woman."

"You realize what a piece of personal furniture might mean to a woman who has traveled all over the world and who doesn't stay in one place long enough to collect—"

"Me? Yes, I realize. She's scared and running now. This might make it worse, but I have to have something to do, other than our remodeling."

"How well I know. I did the same thing when Jessica was trying to make up her mind about me—I made her a desk."

Their father came to stand beside them; Viktor placed an arm around each son and considered the unfinished vanity. "Good for a woman. Hey, Fadey, come see what my son is making for his woman."

Fadey and his sons, Mikhail and Jarek, came to consider the vanity. "Good work. I could use you here in my shop," Fadey said as he passed around the plastic container of his wife's raspberry-filled cookies. In the crowded corner of the shop where Danya had been working, the men settled on unfinished chairs, tabletops and low coffee tables, all built in the sturdy Stepanov style. They ate cookies, considered the type of hardware for the vanity's drawers and Fadey said, "My wife makes these for me. Don't eat too many. They are mine," he teased.

"You know, our women have decided to contact Sidney, if she doesn't return soon," Fadey added. "They may use excuses, but it is really because they want to help you with courting your woman, boy. Perhaps my sons can give little bits of advice."

Viktor placed his open hand on Fadey's broad chest and pushed lightly, teasingly. "Brother, my son knows how to please a woman—look what he is making, a gift of the heart, is it not?"

Fadey smiled widely. "That it is—"

The shop's door opened and Sidney, dressed in a ball cap, a photographer's vest over her T-shirt and cargo pants, her camera-gear bag slung over one shoulder and a sleeping bag over the other was silhouetted in the doorway.

The stack of chairs in front of the men provided a view of Sidney, but prevented her from seeing them clearly. She slung the sleeping bag onto a door braced over two sawhorses and plopped the camera bag on top of it. She scanned the shop, turned off the music and yelled, "Stepanov! Get your butt front and center."

Seated on an unfinished table top, Danya grimly finished his cookie. He should have known that Sidney would skip any advance notice. "Hark. The voice of my angel," he murmured darkly.

Jarek chuckled, Mikhail smothered a grin and the elder Stepanov males smiled widely. "We could hide," Alexi whispered in a staged fearful tone. "She didn't say which Stepanov butt."

Danya scowled at his brother and called coolly to Sidney, "I'm over here, my darling."

He knew exactly how the endearment would hit Sidney. If she didn't think that his family knew that they were lovers, she was very, very wrong. She stopped scanning the expansive shop, and tilted her head to look around the stack of chairs. She stared at the men for a moment.

"Oh, hello," she said lightly, as if she were trying to cover her surprise.

"Don't anyone move. I may need you for protection," Danya murmured dryly.

"But she is so small and cute," Viktor returned in a whisper. "Perfect for a bride. She is small like your mother...she could wear your mother's wedding dress—"

"One word of that and she'll be off and running."

"Run fast after her," Alexi advised softly as Sidney made her way around furniture until she came to them.

She nodded to men, seated on various furniture. "I didn't know you all were here. Jessica said that Danya was working over here and I somehow thought he would be alone— Oh, hi, Danya."

Fadey reached for Sidney, enveloped her in a big hug that left her slightly dazed, and then Viktor hugged her, waggling her slightly from side to side. "Welcome back, Sidney. We missed you."

Released from the affectionate but powerful hugs, Sidney braced her hand onto one table and shook her head slightly as if trying to find her balance. She took the cookie that Fadey pushed into her hand and stared at it. "Thanks."

Danya had been frustrated for eight long days, waiting for her call, a word, anything that said she felt something for what had happened between them, for what could happen. There was just that brief kiss-off phone call in which she stated everything on her mind, and now she just turned up?

She actually thought he'd given her the earrings as payment for sex? For making love with him? Now that Sidney was near and within reach, he wanted to yell at her. But he wouldn't—because no matter how much she irritated him, he was not a yeller. "Hi," he returned coolly as he took the cookie from Sidney and ate it slowly. "What's up?"

"I—I came back…uh…to take the portraits of your family…uh…maybe of the resort, you know, for the new brochure?"

Perhaps it was his brooding Russian blood, but Danya had to have more. "Where are you staying tonight?" he asked too quietly, because she had wounded him deeply. *They had become lovers and she had left him so easily, had suggested that he would pay her for lovemaking, and hadn't contacted him.* She had come back to Amoteh to take pictures of his family and his cousin's resort. But she had not said anything about returning to him.

Sidney's brown eyes widened and blinked. "Huh?"

He'd had to have something to salve his pride, and now she was blushing and looking panicked and helpless. Viktor nudged Danya with his elbow, and Alexi shook his head slightly, warningly, but Danya didn't move. "Stay where you want," he said finally with a light shrug, hoping that she would choose him.

Had he no pride? She had insulted him in several ways and now he was feeling as if he were a brute, kicking a kitten. She'd done that to him, too—made him feel as if he were in the wrong—*and he wasn't. His mother's earrings for sex?*

That was an insult to his honor. But then, what did Sidney know of a man's honor? She just tramped through her own life, hitting and running, leaving him with sleepless nights and an aching heart.

Now Sidney was frowning and moving in close, her hands on her hips and Danya knew she was set to argue. He wasn't the kind to argue either, but right now, with Sidney pushing him, he just might.

"I don't need permission from you for anything, Stepanov," she stated.

The other men had backed slightly away, leaving Danya to fend for himself. He caught his father's disapproving scowl; he had been taught better manners in dealing with women— but then Sidney wasn't any ordinary woman, and Danya was feeling bruised and nasty. "In some things, you do, my darling."

Her lips tightened and her eyes narrowed, indicating that the reminder that he wouldn't be available to her as she wished, but that their lovemaking needed joint approval had sunk home.

Sidney's hand shot out to grip the shirt at his chest and she breathed heavily as if controlling her temper. There was only one way he knew how to deal with Sidney as she stood, scowling up at him. He stood, reached for her, tugged her against him and holding her tight, and fastened his lips to hers. There was just that breath of surprise and then she melted sweetly, slightly against him. Her fingers went to his hair, holding him tight and she stood on tiptoe to meet that hard demanding kiss, serving it back to him with a hunger that said she had missed him, too.

"That's all I wanted to know," he said as he stepped back, studied Sidney's slightly dazed expression and bent to place her over his shoulder. Danya straightened, glanced at his family who were grinning widely. He nodded grimly, and walked toward the door with Sidney who had started to squirm.

She was fast and she was evil and she was sweet and she was the woman he wanted.

All he had to do was to make sense of her and untangle his emotions—no simple thing.

The best thing was to keep walking down to the beach, carrying her on his shoulder, because if he didn't—if he didn't, Danya wasn't certain what combustion could occur between them. He hadn't lost his temper in his life, but this one woman could make him so angry—

"Now you've made me mad, Stepanov. You can't just haul me around like some—some…." Sidney stated in a low warning tone. "Just wait until I get my hands on you."

Danya kept walking until he reached his beachfront home. He shifted Sidney from his shoulder down into his arms. While she was dealing with that sudden change, he opened the door with one hand and eased her through the doorway.

He placed her on her feet, latched one hand to the waistband of her cargo pants and said, "You were saying? Something about getting your hands on me?"

"You're just not nice, Stepanov," she said quietly, dangerously after giving up on prying his grip away from her pants. "People think you are, but you aren't. Not really. You're bossy, irritating, and…and well, something else, too, but right now, I can't think of any more to say, because I am so mad at you."

"That's good. Let it all out," he ordered grimly, "It's been one week since that little kiss-off call, and days before that there was nothing. Not a word from you. Did you think for one minute that might have bothered me?"

Sidney blinked several times and then in a very small voice, she said, "No?"

Well, this wasn't going well at all, Sidney decided as Danya loomed over her, his big fist gripping the waistband of her pants.

"You didn't think that remark about my mother's earrings as payment for sex would insult me?"

Sidney did that stunned, blinking and blank expression that said she hadn't considered that she might nick his honor. "No?" she questioned again in a very small voice.

Danya was on a roll and he wasn't stopping. Like it or not,

in a lover-situation, Sidney needed to know that she couldn't just waltz off with his heart and not suffer the consequences of hearing what she had done. "So you just thought you would dip into Amoteh, take a few payback pictures, because you're obligated, et cetera, and return the earrings to me, right?"

"Um…sort of." She wasn't too certain what her plan had been, other to take photographs of the Stepanovs and maybe sneak one of Danya that she could keep and remember him when she was far, far away and crying over him and thinking of how he had made long, sweet love to her. She'd planned to complete her obligation to Ellie for sewing the lovely gown so quickly, and she'd needed to see that Danya was safe and not thinking of cliffs and jumping.

Sidney changed her mind—yes, she did know what her plan was, and it was for closure in both their lives.

"Get this: I never planned to jump off any cliff, and I'm not Ben," Danya was saying darkly.

"You're telling me," Sidney returned hotly. "*He* would never have been so—so rude. *He* would have never yelled at me, or packed me around in front of everyone. And he sure would never have planted that—that kiss on me that made me forget everything I'd planned to do. He would have never, ever have done anything so—so—I still can't place just how awful that was, to just flat out show your relatives that we—that we had one…uh…occasion, a you-know-what. Ben was a gentleman," she finished adamantly.

"I never yelled at you, though the urge is there. You could make anyone yell."

"You did the same as yell. You had that too quiet tone and you looked dangerous, like some pirate or something. Yes, that's what you acted like, a dangerous pirate carrying me about like some—how medieval, how neanderthal. Men just don't do that anymore. You've got all these old-fashioned ideas that no one has anymore."

"Do tell. That we are lovers and I want to act like it and expect some small courtesy from you to acknowledge that we did make love—not sex, dear heart—is something you can't understand?"

"You're definitely not getting the picture here, Stepanov. We don't fit, get it? You, traditional and romantic...me, a woman on the move. I feel like I'm being netted into something that scares the holy hell out of me. And I think I'm really mad about you leading me on that first bit, when I thought you might really want to dive over that cliff. Now that wasn't nice, was it? Not that I want you to be a jumper."

She was pacing and waving her hands now, turning to periodically glare at him. His anger cooling at the sight, Danya considered the emotional woman in front of him. Sidney was definitely a passionate woman, despite her claims of being an "observer of life." She was definitely involved in their relationship, or she wouldn't be all flushed and furious. Sidney was fighting mad, but was it at him alone? Was a part of it because she loved him and didn't know how to handle their love? "So my kiss can stop your mind. It's like the rest of you, very agile and very fast. Hmm, now I wonder what that means?" he asked quietly, thoughtfully.

"Oh, darn," she said as the impact of his statement hit her. Her anger melted into that soft feeling that needed to be wrapped up in Danya's strong arms. Her eyes burned and she sniffed, a sign that her tears weren't far away. That dreaded weakness hadn't occurred until she'd met Danya, over two weeks ago. "Okay, we're sexually attracted. Like magnets, or something. I don't know why. But I do know that you seemed easygoing and friendly and now you're all different."

"Because I have the status of being your lover, my darling."

"Lover?" The word hit Sidney broadside.

"And you are mine. But there is more than sex involved here, dear heart."

"There is?"

But then Danya moved slowly toward her and she didn't have time to mull all the reasons why Danya shouldn't love her, and why they weren't suited, and why a relationship between them wouldn't work. Well, okay. A sexual relationship would work, but other than an infrequent hit-and-run, it would be disastrous.

She backed away one step, then another, and extended her hand out protectively in front of her. Danya's chest came against her palm and she backed away another step. Those dark blue eyes had locked onto her face, lowered to her lips, and then slid to study her breasts. That intent, purposeful look took her breath away, started her body simmering and aching, and she fought the quiver running through her as she stared at the lips she wanted to kiss—

"Oh, Sidney," Danya whispered as his finger stroked her cheek. "You're blushing again."

"I'm just out of breath. Being hauled around like a bag of—"

Her back came against the door and Danya's big hands flattened on the wood beside her head. His thumbs caressed her earlobes and her senses started vibrating warily, telling her that in one heartbeat, she could be on him and feasting on that gorgeous mouth—

He was an intent sort of guy, Sidney reminded herself, and set on a course, Danya was very thorough. He was watching her now, as if he could see all the little hot impulses, the fear inside her. "So you came back to take pictures of my family and the resort. And that's all? Or did you come back to finish it between us?" he asked too softly.

"You're yelling again," she whispered, because she sensed just how dangerous he could be when aroused to anger. "Okay, I'm sorry about the earrings-for-sex remark. Back off, will you? You're crowding me."

"I've crowded you before. You didn't mind it then. Can't you deal with this, Sidney? A discussion of our relationship?"

Both of her hands were on his broad powerful chest now, and Danya was leaning very close, his head tilted so that he could nuzzle the side of her throat. "Tell me, Sidney. You came back just for the pictures, right? And how is good old Ben?"

His lips were near hers, playing at the sensitive corners now. Sidney was trying desperately to concentrate on what he had just asked when all she wanted to do was to dive into his kiss and devour him. "Are you going to kiss me or not?"

His lips smoothed hers, rubbing slightly. "You're very hot, Sidney. Could it be that you're aroused by me? Did you miss me?"

She gave him that. "Maybe. Just maybe I did."

His tongue flicked at her lips, his body pressing close to hers, and she wanted to inhale him. "So then, just maybe— just maybe you came back to see me, too?"

"You scare me…."

"I know." His light kisses were tempting her now, roaming over her lips, never stopping, never letting her take what she wanted….

Sidney opened her lips, met his tongue with hers and let the taste of him flow warmly, sensuously through her. "Okay, I missed you."

"How? As a friend? As a lover?"

"Just you. I missed you."

"Good. That's all I wanted to know—" Then Danya pushed away and walked from her into the bathroom. "I'm going to Uncle Fadey and Aunt Mary Jo's for dinner. My family will all be there. You can come, if you want. The food is good."

Sidney caught her breath. One minute Danya was so close and sensual and the next he was treating her as if she was a casual acquaintance—and she wasn't! They'd made love after all, very satisfying love. On unsteady legs, she walked to the bathroom and studied Danya, who was shaving. He'd removed his shirt and his tanned bare chest gleamed in the room's bald light. The white foam on his jaw did not soften the hard set of it, that muscle contracting in his throat.

"You're really, really mad, aren't you?" she asked.

In the mirror, those hard blue eyes slashed at her as he took a brief stroke with his straight razor. "Of course. It never should have happened that way between us."

The hair on Sidney's nape lifted warningly. "What do you mean?"

"I took you too soon. You deserved more. And so did I."

"You mean you regret having sex with me?"

He swished his straight razor in the basin of water. "Yes, I do. I'm not made for a one-night stand and neither are you."

He had qualms about their lovemaking! Stunned that he would regret something so lovely, Sidney considered her options. Danya had asked if she would run and accused her of being afraid. He seemed engrossed in shaving and she needed his full attention. Small and agile had its advantages she decided, as she wiggled to stand in front of him. Those blue eyes glanced down at her and then looked over her head to the mirror as he continued to shave.

"Sure, I'd love to come to dinner. Thanks. Let's get back to the part about you and I shouldn't have had sex."

Danya nodded just once and reached around her to swish his straight razor again. He looked down at her briefly, then straightened. "I should have had more control than to take you so quickly. But then, you were missing dear old Ben, weren't you? Or were you playing at revenge? Getting back at him by having me?"

Sidney tensed; she now suspected that she'd hurt Danya even more deeply than she'd realized. "Look, I wanted you. I nailed you. It's just that simple. I'm sorry if I hurt your feelings. I guess at the time, I was just feeling the moment and greedy and maybe wanting— I'm used to moving fast in situations and well, there you were, all warmed up and ready."

"You think you can just 'nail' a man and run away the next morning?"

"I did not 'run away,' you caught me on the beach. You were naked, remember? And I had a job to do back in New York. I came back to return those earrings in person, didn't I?"

"They were a gift with no strings attached. Where are they?"

This truthful conversation was getting rougher and more intricate by the moment. She hadn't realized that Danya would be so sensitive, so vulnerable. Or so—tough and cold. She dug down into her cargo pants pocket and extracted a small box with a rubber band wrapped around it. She had to give the earrings back—they were a family heirloom and she had no right to them. But they were so beautiful— Sidney took a deep steadying breath and placed them on a shelf with his shaving kit. "Here they are. Now we're even."

His "Are we?" was too tight as he continued shaving.

"Yes, I think so. I think we're about as even as we can get."

His jaw tightened at that, but he kept stroking the razor across his skin. The slight scraping sound raised the hair on her nape again. "Get out of here, Sidney."

"I'm not budging until you admit that I am not a coward and—"

"Have you ever made love in a bathroom yet? You're shocked, aren't you? I guess that means you haven't. So unless you want to—now—leave."

"Boy, you're cranky," Sidney stated as she eased away and Danya's narrowed eyes followed her. She glanced down to the bulge in his jeans and decided that he was perfectly capable of making love whenever he wanted.

His look was dark and fierce as he reached to close the door in her face.

"You're sure not sweet," she stated to the closed door. She couldn't let Danya treat her so lightly and opened the door, entering the bathroom. "Give me those earrings. I wouldn't insult something so precious by leaving them with you."

Danya tossed the small box to her. "Is there anything else you want, dearest?"

For a moment, the response that she wanted to make love to him in any room, on any flat plane available, lingered on her lips. Then she decided a retreat was wiser at the moment, until they both had time to reason and chose their words. "Nope, not a thing."

She closed the bathroom door behind her, and with shaking hands attached the earrings. Then because the shower was running and she could only think of the naked body in the spray of water, all hard and thrusting and hot and full and—Sidney stepped out into the cool salty Pacific night. On the porch were her sleeping and camera bags; in the distance, Alexi turned and waved.

"Thanks," she called and laden with her things, stepped back into the cabin. Sidney unrolled her sleeping bag to remove her clothing within and her small traveling bag. She stood and noted the gown she'd worn at the soiree; it hung against the wall, looking sleek and feminine and unlike anything she would wear. Sidney moved to it and smoothed the soft black fabric with her fingers; she remembered how tenderly and carefully Danya had touched her, wooed her until they moved together naturally....

She hadn't "nailed him." They'd made love together, and just maybe he had a right to be angry. Men were very complicated, Sidney decided; they had funny little vulnerable pieces that needed soothing.

She slowly unlaced her boots, removed them and her socks, and then stripped away her shirt, preparing to change into clean clothing for dinner. She had removed her sports bra and was just sliding away her pants when Danya stepped into the room wearing only the towel around his hips.

His dark stare instantly pinned and held her, poised just so with her hands gripping her pants at her knees. She refused to be intimidated by that hot hungry look, by the ripples it sent through her body. She wasn't a coward and she wouldn't run. She released her pants to the floor, stepped out of them and straightened bravely to face him.

"Do you think I could be aroused by just any woman?" he asked softly, sensuously, dangerously as he took in the sight of her rigid body. "Was it that easy for you to have me and walk away?"

"I thought you were a friend and a nice guy. I was having a moment, okay? Do you really regret that night? With me?"

Danya was too close now and his finger rose to gently flip

the earring. "That I claimed you for my own? No. I took you to the display room to cool you down, dear heart, and then—"

"Wait a minute. Repeat that: You 'claimed' me?"

Danya's hand slid slowly down her throat, over her chest and smoothed her breasts. Her reaction was automatic, her hands locking on his arms; he wasn't going anywhere. His gaze was lowering, skimming her body, those blue eyes flickering, and the tense hot moments sprung between them. "I want you," Danya admitted. "But I also want more. I almost came after you. If I had, the result wouldn't have been nice and it wouldn't have settled anything."

Sidney shook her head, trying to understand. "Why would you come after me?"

His thumbs caressed her nipples and he moved close and tight, bending to kiss her hard and hot. Sidney stood on tiptoe, wrapped her arms around his neck and held tight, diving into the kiss, meeting him. Skin against skin, she met the blunt nudge of his sex with her hips and then Danya's hands were beneath her bottom, lifting her. Sidney couldn't wait, agilely raising herself and wrapping her legs around him, fastening her lips to his, taking in the heat from his body. "Sidney…." Danya cautioned roughly. "We're not protected."

She moved to taste his ear and nibble on his jaw. Danya was so tastable. "You should buy a big carton."

His smile slid against her cheek. "Why? Is this going to happen often?"

"Do you have to talk now?" Sidney wanted to move into the real action.

"No, but I do like you talking when we're like this. It's very…erotic."

She stopped tasting him and leaned back to study his expression. "Me? Erotic?"

"Sexy."

She traced his lashes, the silky feel in contrast to the hard bones of his face. He was sweet and boyish in his way, despite the all male feel of him against her, almost within her.

She kissed him once, just lightly, tasting the new tenderness between them, and Danya lowered her to her feet.

He still held her as she considered this new sensation, sweet and soft and slow. Sidney lay against him, placing her head upon his shoulder. She felt so safe in his arms, and well—feminine and new. "This is a good feeling. But I like sex with you, too."

"That's good."

"Just so you know—I'm not a girly-girly kind of woman. I'm not going to hold you to anything, or throw a fit if you see someone you—"

Danya placed his hand over her lips. "Let's just go to dinner, okay?"

"Put me down," Sidney ordered as Danya carried her up the steps to Fadey and Mary Jo Stepanov's home.

Danya seemed determined to hold her, despite her wriggling in his arms, and he grimly ignored her as he stood in front of the double wide wooden doors of the sprawling Stepanov home. Sidney gave up trying to free herself and asked, "Do I look all right? I mean, the last time your brother and cousins and uncle saw me, they saw me being packed out of the shop by you. I'd like to make a better impression on them."

"You look fine. Your work boots add a lot to the look."

"The heels were just borrowed and I don't have anything else."

His eyes skimmed the square bodice of her long black gown and for a moment, time spun around Sidney, slowed and stopped as Danya bent to slowly, effectively kiss her.

"Mmm—" Sidney gave herself to the hard warmth of his lips, to the flick of his tongue, her internal motors turning up.

Just then, the door opened and Fadey and Viktor stood together, grinning at the sight of Sidney in Danya's arms. "Um," Sidney began nervously and realized she was blushing again. "Um," she managed again and then gave up any explanation of why Danya was holding her.

"Welcome to my home," Fadey said warmly, stepping back for Danya to enter with Sidney.

Viktor's expression was soft and filled with love. "My son."

"I don't weigh much. He's not hurting his back," Sidney said hurriedly. "He's pretty strong, you know. And he seems to like to pack things around. I don't know why."

"I know." Viktor took Sidney's hand and kissed the back of it with an old world elegance.

"Put me down," Sidney whispered again to Danya as she noted the rest of his family in the spacious living room.

He wasn't paying attention but watching his aunt come from the kitchen. Mary Jo, a long-legged former Texan, smiled warmly at Sidney and came to nestle in Fadey's arms.

"Hello, darlin'," Mary Jo said. "We're glad you could come. Put her down, Danya. She's embarrassed, poor thing."

When Danya placed Sidney on her feet, she frowned at him. "Oh, now you put me down."

Mary Jo took her hand and walked into the large living room with her. A massive stone fireplace dominated the room, the huge windows overlooked the ocean, and the sturdy Stepanov furniture, the wooden wall panels all created a beautiful, comfortable setting. Thick, serviceable rugs crossed the gleaming hardwood floors, and pottery in shades of earth, sea and sky softened the room.

Jarek, Alexi and Mikhail stood when she entered the room and the women greeted her with warm smiles.

She'd never really been in a family setting—where she was a lover of a man of the family, therefore, a pseudo-family member herself. Now that was terrifying. If Danya continued as he had been, those children playing with that massive dollhouse could include her own—

Babies. Home. Things she'd never known.... Terrified that she was entering an unfamiliar realm, Sidney backed up and found Danya's body. His arms went around her waist drawing her close, and she felt instantly safe. Danya always felt safe, she realized, even when he was angry. "Danya?"

He leaned down so she could whisper in his ear. "I don't want to hold any kids, okay? That's what people usually do, stick babies in my arms and I don't know what to do with them."

"Okay," he whispered back, then he announced, "Sidney is afraid to hold babies. Don't make her take them—uh!" Her elbow nudged his ribs, stopping any more humiliation.

Viktor was chuckling aloud. "Give me that girl," he said, reaching for Sidney and wrapping her in a bear hug that took away her breath and lifted her feet off the ground. "You remind me of my dear wife, Sara," he said. "Small, perfect, beautiful. She gave me two strong sons, you know," he announced proudly. "You have boys in your family?"

"Just Stretch and Junior, my sisters."

"I hope you like Tex-Mex food, darlin'," Mary Jo said, taking Sidney's hand and leading her to the spacious kitchen. "I saw some of your work. You've got the eye to capture natural expressions. No wonder the models loved you so. You caught them at their best—they told me so."

"I did?" Sidney turned to look back at Danya, who was watching her with that shielded, dark intent look that said he wanted her staked out beneath him. After that, she barely noticed the spacious tile-lined kitchen with its pottery and hanging strands of red chili peppers.

As the family prepared to take their places at the massive, long walnut table, and Danya came to stand beside her. With a glance, he indicated where she was to sit. Since there was an empty chair next to hers, and Mikhail was already seated, Sidney pulled out Danya's chair. With a long sigh and a wry look around the table, he sat slowly. "Thank you."

Sidney sat beside him. The family was talking, a steady energetic buzz of settling children around the table.

"I'm overdressed," she whispered to Danya as she noted that the other women were wearing cotton summer dresses.

He drew her hand to his thigh and held it as he leaned to

kiss her cheek. "But you're beautiful and you're wearing a gift from Ellie."

Startled by his open show of affection, Sidney shielded her blush. "Don't do that again, Stepanov."

He toyed with her earring and kissed her ear. She frowned up at him. Her "You're pushing your luck, buster" statement landed in the middle of a very quiet moment, when all the Stepanovs had suddenly stopped talking.

Viktor erupted in roaring laughter, so much that tears came to his eyes. "So like my Sara," he managed, dabbing his eyes with a napkin.

Ellie seemed to understand Sidney's embarrassment and reached across Mikhail to touch her arm. "I'm so pleased you wore the dress I made. I feel honored. I love to sew. Mikhail made me the most beautiful sewing cabinet, and you've got to come see my sewing room."

"And my office," Mary Jo added. "Okay, everyone. Let's eat."

After dinner, the family moved into the living room, and Danya drew Sidney to sit on his lap. "Room economy," he explained with a devastating grin.

"Sure," she returned, disbelieving him because she had noted several empty seating places on the long gorgeous couches. She also noted Jessica sitting on Alexi's lap, Leigh on Jarek's, and Ellie on Mikhail's. The women, comfortable with their husbands, snuggled close and the couples spoke intimately, clearly in love.

Sidney inhaled, noted how Danya's eyes went instantly to her breasts, and held her breath. Beneath her, Danya's body was thrusting and hard, his hands open on her body, drawing her close. "Don't move," he whispered unevenly in her ear. "You're not wearing any—"

She released her breath and decided to pay him back for packing her out of the shop. She wiggled slightly and smiled smugly up at him. "No panties. Mess with me, will you? Take that," she whispered.

"Oh, you're going to…"

* * *

"Dinner was nice. Lots of family. Beautiful home…loved the landscapes of Texas, all the fields and cattle," Sidney summarized as they walked along the beach.

Danya caught the underlying uncertainty in her tone. "And it scared you. You didn't relax until after dinner."

"And only then, because the food was so good and I was getting drowsy…. You're wasting your time with me, Danya. I'm not going to fit into this picture. I've never lived in one place in my entire lifetime."

"I'm not asking you anything. We're enjoying each other, aren't we?"

"No. Not always. At the shop, you showed a very nasty, snarly side. I'm not usually put into the position of trying to smooth things. Either they are, or they aren't. No offense, but you're a relationship kind of guy, a deep one. Too deep. You take things and turn them and think about them. A very hard-to-read kind of guy, brooding, sort of. I take life as it comes and if I don't like it, I move on. And you yelled at me—sort of, I took it as yelling anyway."

"Are those my good points?"

In the moonlight with the waves rolling onto shore behind her, Sidney turned to look up at him. "It's all those moody angles that I don't understand. I still haven't gotten over being packed out of that shop over your shoulder. I mean how much dignity in that is there? I'm a professional, after all."

"So are you going to stay with me? While you're here?" he asked as he smoothed that wisp of hair from her cheek. It slid silkily upon his skin before the wind took it away, just as Sidney's assignments could take her away from him.

"I could stay at the resort until the portraits are done. I've worked out deals before—maybe Mikhail would trade a room there for the work done on his brochure. There's always lots of bartering in this business. Your aunt's brochures are lovely, so is the Stepanov Furniture. I could probably stay with your aunt and uncle."

He bent to brush her lips with his, tasting the hunger there. "That would embarrass me."

"How so?"

"I'd come to you, and I haven't crawled into a bedroom window for years."

"Oh." Sidney looked out onto the black waves, the shimmering, silvery trail of moonlight coming across them.

Danya took her face in his hands, turning it up to him. "Now who's thinking too much?" he asked gently before kissing her. He lifted her into his arms and carried her toward his cabin. "I like this," Danya whispered as he carried her inside and closed the door.

"I haven't figured out how I like it—being carried around—but it sure is taking a long time to get you onto that bed."

"I'm seducing you, dear heart. I don't want you to get any wrong ideas about payment later, either."

"Sorry about that. I know that hurt your feelings. It's just that I didn't have anything to give you." She was still high in his arms, holding him and kissing him, giving those little hungry noises from deep inside her throat.

"You bring me peace and warmth and pleasure and friendship. Those are very special gifts that I haven't had for a very long time."

Sidney felt a piece of her heart tear softly away. "With your wife. She must have been wonderful."

"She was. We were young and life waited for us, the adventure of it."

Sidney snuggled against him. She'd never been a cuddler, but Danya was perfect for it. She loved to touch him, to run her fingers through his waving hair, to look into those sky-blue eyes and feel his skin against hers, his hands upon her. "You'll find someone and get that home and children, Danya. But I'm glad that we're together now."

"Oh, I intend to get what I want. What I need," he said firmly as he carried her to the bed.

Seven

The next morning, Sidney took film out of her photographer's vest, reloaded her camera and prepared to take shots of the Amoteh Resort's Russian style *samovar,* a huge, beautiful ornate device for brewing and serving tea. Intended for bridal showers and elegant social affairs, the Amoteh's Tea Room was definitely feminine, with cream and cabbage rose draperies and small groupings of tables and chairs. Each table was covered by a cloth decorated with strawberries, the Amoteh logo, with a beautiful tumble of fresh roses in the center. The soft light filtering into the Amoteh's Tea Room caught the Old World elegance in a soothing blend of dark red and cream hues. Mikhail's wife and his sometimes assistant, Ellie, had prepared the serving table setting for the shoot, complete with the traditional Russian glasses in ornate meal holders. Mary Jo had baked the raspberry-filled cookies for the tray, and Sidney had arranged the delicate cloth napkins next to a small dish heaped with strawberries.

Dressed in a sleek business suit, Mikhail stood in the shadows, his arms crossed as he watched Ellie and Sidney prepare the shots. Jarek had just come to check on the Stepanov Furniture display room and watched with interest.

Absorbed in her craft, Sidney snapped pictures quickly. She moved around the serving table for better shots, backed into someone and heard a masculine grunt. Irritated that someone had caused her to lose focus and the shot, she pivoted quickly. "Listen, bud. I'm working here. Just keep out of my way, will you?"

She looked the long way up to Danya's pleased grin. The huge bouquet of red roses he held between them startled her. "For you, my darling."

He bent to kiss her and then straightened, that devastating boyish grin widening as he held the bouquet out to her.

Stunned, Sidney gripped her camera. She'd never had a bouquet before. "There must be some mistake. You already gave me a flower, an orchid. I still have it. Oh, it's all flat now, squashed between the pages of a coffee table book I did on India, but it's still good."

"These are fresh."

Sidney carefully placed her camera on a table, removed her light meter from her neck and took the bouquet. They were beautiful and fragrant and in an obviously old tall, cut glass vase. "What do I do with them? What are they for?"

"For you," Danya said quietly as he removed one bud, shortened the stem and tucked it over her ear.

She'd heard of other women receiving roses after a romantic, sensual night and understood the gesture immediately, which brought a blush to her cheeks.

It seemed only right that she give him something, too, so Sidney placed the vase on a table and took a rosebud. She carefully shortened the stem as he had done and then stood on tiptoe to tuck it over his ear. She leaned close to whisper, "Thanks for last night, but really, this wasn't necessary."

Then because he looked so pleased with himself, so tall and beautiful and sweet, Sidney removed another bud from the bouquet and placed that one over his other ear. "Thank you," Danya whispered unevenly. "I'd better let you get back to work."

Sidney gripped his cotton shirt in her fist; she couldn't let him go. She turned to the Stepanovs who were all smiling softly, just as they had at the calendar windup party. While she tried to think of an explanation of why Danya had given her the roses, he whispered huskily, "See you tonight."

Danya picked up a juicy strawberry and slowly placed it in her mouth; she returned the favor automatically, fascinated by that hard masculine mouth. It slowly curved into a pleased smile and then he turned to walk out of the room. He was whistling; the Stepanovs were smiling softly at her.

Her heart started to beat again and tears burned her eyes. "I…I think I need a break," she murmured unevenly as she picked up a delicate napkin and blew her nose on it. "I must be getting a cold. Or maybe it's allergies."

Or just maybe—she hurried after Danya.

She caught him in the hallway near the furniture display room. Surprised, Danya turned, caught her as she leaped upon him, her arms around his neck. With her in his arms, Danya pivoted and entered the display room, closing the door behind him.

"Do you have to be so difficult?" she asked against his lips.

"Who, me?"

"Now how am I going to top that bouquet?" she asked as she pushed him back onto the display bed and came down upon him. Entranced with the rugged man beneath her, the way his blue eyes looked up tenderly at her, Sidney smoothed his hair back from his face. The soft moment clung between them—not sexual, but gentle and sweet. "You look good in rosebuds, Danya."

"I planted the bushes this morning. The blooms made me think of you."

"I'm more of a cactus person, don't you think?"

"No, you're definitely a rose in full bloom, with maybe a few daisies in the mix." His big hand was doing that smoothing thing on her head, like petting, she decided as she leaned into it.

Was it so wrong to want these perfect moments, to store them inside? Sidney wondered as she snuggled close and safe to Danya. She would probably finish shooting the Stepanovs within the week. "I should go."

"Stay," Danya whispered against her lips. "Or I'll have to come after you."

"You'd do that?"

"I would."

A week, no more, Sidney promised herself as she slid over Danya. In the predawn, he was still sleeping and thus perfect for a fast take. He'd probably sleep through the whole thing and never realize that she needed him once again after the two times they'd shared during the night. She'd make love with him so many times in the next week that he'd never forget her. She'd have those memories to take with her into the long hot safaris and cold Arctic nights. Taking the opportunity for good natural shots had given her expertise in recognizing the right moment—

The right moment had occurred immediately after she'd entered the cabin last night, carrying her precious rose bouquet. Danya had been cooking, and he'd turned to her with a smile that had stilled slowly as their eyes had met and their sensual hunger began. He'd turned off the stove and Sidney had placed the beautiful vase onto the table. Dinner had been a long time later.

Now, lying beside her, Danya was hard and perfect and sweet and her fever for him was running high. She closed her eyes as she slid upon him, bracing her weight apart, holding him tight and full within her. She moved slightly, experimentally, not wanting to wake him.

Then drawn by the beauty of his face, those long eyelashes, those fierce brows, those sensuous lips, Sidney paused to study him. She smoothed away the waving hair from his cheek, considered the hard shape of his jaw, the texture of his early morning stubble rough against her fingertip. She'd remember him forever, a picture locked in her mind of a man she'd once known, and had cherished.

Sidney frowned slightly. But a relationship like those she'd seen in the Stepanov family, the men teasing, the women's seductive looks, that quiet, sharing loving clearly seen between them?

A week was best. Just a perfect little time capsule to draw out and remember—she placed her lips on his, brushing them lightly, and Danya's blue eyes opened slightly and his expression was wry. "Having fun?"

"Yes, and you're supposed to be sleeping."

His hands raised to smooth her hips, bringing her closer. "I like to do my share. You could get pregnant this way, you know—without protection."

That thought surprised her. Sidney hadn't thought of herself as a mother, of a child growing within her, yet at the moment, that possibility didn't frighten her. The need to capture a part of Danya, a beautiful little child, fascinated her. But then that child should belong to a woman who could give him everything—

Sidney had lived a lifestyle where she took what she could get at the moment, and Danya was very much at the moment. "I thought I'd be gone before you got serious."

"Ah. I see. Hit and run."

She left her body flow into his hands, his caresses over her already sensitized breasts. "This is nice, talking like this during sex."

Danya's strained expression said that he was fighting his desire. "Just don't move. I don't trust myself with you. The thought of you carrying my child is very, very erotic."

Sidney allowed herself to be placed aside momentarily and then Danya drew her back astride him, his hands on her hips, urging her into position, moving her gently, rhythmically over him. "You were saying?"

He'd stunned her, the position new and exciting. "I can't think now. Later," Sidney managed as she gave herself into the pleasured race and felt her body clenching his—

She was just falling gently when Danya turned her easily, coming over her. "Oh, Sidney," he singsonged softly against her cheek.

"Mmm. What?" She fought to drag herself up from the warm limp blissful bog. "Oh, yeah, right. There's your part, huh?"

"Something like that." Danya took his time, tasting her body, suckling gently at her breasts, nibbling on them, and moving slowly within her. "What do you want to talk about?"

"I can't think of anything at the moment." Sidney's body was already hitting those pleasured peaks again, and she held him with all her strength, her fingers digging into his shoulders. Passion rose hungrily within her, driven by the rough sound of his breathing, the heat of his face against her, his lips burning her flesh, his hand— She tried to capture the need within her, keeping all the pleasure tight and safe and then it came bursting—

That high keening sound was her own, shocking, female, desperate. It echoed around her, even as Danya tensed, his expression fierce as he gave himself to her. He was damp and heavy, and she couldn't let him move away. "I—I think I bit you. I may have—ah, held you a little too tight. I'm pretty strong, you know."

Against her throat, he murmured, "You did at the last. That's why I couldn't wait any longer."

"Oh, I'm so sorry. I— Oh, Danya. I've lost all control. I'm loud, too. Oh, I am mortified."

"Hush," Danya whispered softly as he kissed her. "Let's just enjoy the moment, okay? So what are your plans for the day?"

She was thinking that lovemaking a few times would be nice. "I thought I'd call around and see who in your family was available for pictures today. What are you going to do?"

He eased aside and lay facing her. He studied the movement of his hand skimming over her body, resting on her hip. "Work. We're almost finished with remodeling. We're starting on another project pretty soon. We could have lunch together."

"Sounds good." The dawn was filling the shadows now and

his shoulder gleamed—the place where she'd bitten him darker than his tanned skin.

She smoothed it with her fingertips and wondered how a man could be so beautiful and powerful and exciting as he lay beside quietly her.

Danya's eyes darkened. "Don't worry, Sidney. Everything is perfectly normal. You're a passionate woman. Come here…."

"You're a cuddler, aren't you?" she murmured as he held her against him and she listened to the steady beat of his heart.

"You're perfect for cuddling."

"You're awfully big for that. I mean, really big. There's no way I can return the favor."

"Mmm. Have I asked?"

In a few moments, Danya eased from the bed and went to take his shower. She could still feel him holding her, his body tight against hers and the scent of their lovemaking settled around her. She held his pillow and sleepily watched him dress for work. Danya came to the bed, studied her and in the silence, his eyes locked with hers. "If I don't leave now—" His voice was grim before he walked to the door.

He turned suddenly, and she lay quietly as the impact of his hunger slid across the room; then Danya stepped into the bright sunlight, closing the door behind him. Sidney lay in his bed, tangled in her emotions and the bed clothing.

The thought of you carrying my child is very, very erotic. From a family such as the Stepanovs, Danya was probably in a biological nesting mode. Sidney lay warm and sated and ran her hands over her very sensitive breasts and then lower to press upon her flat stomach. She lingered in the thought of his child growing within her for just a heartbeat before shaking her head. "It would never work."

Things were working out well, Danya decided two days later in the second week of July. He placed his clothes and Sidney's into the new washer he'd just installed in his newly purchased house—a house that had just popped up on the market and that Sidney didn't know he had purchased.

Her clothing ran to T-shirts, jeans and cargo pants. The morning light coming from the window fell upon the various sports bras hanging to dry above the washer. Danya realized how much he loved to cup her breasts, to feel that delicate weight, to taste those tiny mauve nubs.

He added detergent with the pleased thought that she seemed perfectly settled into Amoteh. She used her laptop to answer e-mail in the manager's suite at the Amoteh Resort. She had taken pictures of the individual families and of the resort, and had snapped photos of the new Stepanov Furniture designs.

But Sidney had mourned the lack of a dark room where she could develop her film. She'd explained the dream of hers to do her own print work by hand; traveling had made a permanent base for that impossible.

Danya walked out of the laundry room and surveyed his barren, unfinished new home. The family who had contracted Stepanov Building Company had just inherited a rich 150-acre farm in northern Missouri and had moved immediately. Danya had purchased this house at a good price and the Stepanovs had kept his secret from Sidney. She was still nervous of their growing relationship and he didn't want to damage any progress by adding to her fears.

He moved into the large room overlooking the Pacific Ocean. Brilliant morning sunlight poured into the room, laying a square pattern on the hard wood flooring.

Comfortable in the oceanside cabin now, Sidney would be terrified if she knew that he planned to make it their home, and that in addition to the rose garden he'd started, he'd already begun counters and cabinets in a former walk-in closet; it would make a perfect dark room. Another well-lighted room would be perfect for a business center and her computer and graphic work.

Danya listened to the hum of the washer and settled in to

imagine life with Sidney, maybe children…. Clearly Sidney loved travel and her work, and Danya had resolved that he would settle for the times she would return to him.

Her exquisite stories were filled with world travel, adventure and Ben, of course. Her former lover had been so much a part of her life and Danya understood the friendship they had shared; however, he was still uncomfortable about their sexual hit and runs and the way Sidney had expected little from a man.

Leashing his plans for marriage wasn't easy, but he would. Until the time was right—

Sidney stared at the lovely set of china that Jessica Stepanov had placed on a lovely round walnut table. "It's beautiful."

A hostess, comfortable in her own home, Jessica poured tea into the ornate cup and handed the saucer to Sidney. "It was Alexi and Danya's mother's. I thought it would make a lovely picture for the family album you're creating for us. By the way, did you like that vase Danya gave you? It was his mother's, too."

"It is?" She'd left it on the cabin table where anything could happen to it.

"It's beautiful, isn't it? It's the baby's nap time and I'm dying for tea and conversation."

"You ran a corporation once, and now you're happy with being a wife and a mother?" Sidney asked, intrigued by Jessica's change from a top-notch executive running her deceased husband's company to Alexi's wife, pleased with her home and family.

Jessica sipped her tea and then said, "Perfectly. There are business things now and then, but basically I walked away from everything. I hadn't known I could be so happy. And I have my own work here, shuttling the elderly to their appointments when my friend, Willow, is busy… Alexi secretly loves the times I do that, because he can just sit and hold Dani through her nap time, rather than putting her in her crib. Oh, here, I want to show you something. I thought perhaps you could do something with this, too, if it's not too much trouble."

She lifted a basket that was on the table closer and opened the lid. "This was Alexi and Danya's mother's patching basket. I feel so selfish hoarding such an heirloom, and if you could somehow use these things with our family portraits, that would be wonderful—something for all of our children to enjoy. I love to embroider, to make Louise's designs come to life. Look—"

Jessica carefully unfolded the clothing on the table, embroidered with flowers and obviously treasured. "This was Alexi's when he was a boy. Look at Louise's beautiful embroidery...see how intricate the vines are, the tiny flowers. Ellie created a perfect replica for the men's festival shirts and all of our husbands have embroidery on them—Alexi wore his to our wedding. It was traditional and beautiful. Danya's isn't embroidered yet."

Sidney remembered Danya noting the same thing. "Well, that's not fair."

Jessica smiled softly. "Because he's not married. His wife or sweetheart might want to do that for him. We didn't want to take that away from the woman who loves him."

"Oh." Sidney ran her hand over the smooth, obviously cherished fabric. She could just imagine Danya as a little boy, wearing his shirt. "He loved his wife so much. I'm so sorry she didn't survive. Jeannie, wasn't it?"

"Yes. But you're good for him."

Sidney shrugged lightly. "I'm not staying. I've never stayed this long in one place before and I need to leave within a week. I'm almost finished here."

She'd promised herself that she would leave soon, and now she was already delaying leaving Danya.... "I'll bring that vase to you for safekeeping, and then someday, Danya may want to give it to someone else."

Jessica sipped her tea and said quietly, "Don't pass this by, Sidney, not without really trying."

"We're so opposite. I'm not used to being surrounded by family, or the little homey, everyday things you and the other women here do—and Danya is all about family and home. And he hasn't met my family yet."

She shuddered mentally at the thought of Bulldog, Stretch and Junior arriving in Amoteh. If Bulldog discovered that she had been actually living with Danya, he would come to Amoteh and ruin everything.

Jessica's hand enclosed Sidney's. "Don't worry so, Sidney. Just take it as it comes, day by day. But I am certain that Danya can handle anything your family delivers. I hear that Fadey is really pleased with the pictures you took of his new dining room table and chair designs and Mary Jo is busy working up a new brochure. We really appreciate you taking pictures of our family, in all the different groupings we've asked for—it's going to be a wonderful album. Do you think you can incorporate these things, the china and embroidery into some of the portraits?"

Sidney's mind was already designing layouts: Jessica holding her baby, rocking in a sturdy Stepanov chair, the embroidery basket nearby.

Then she thought of the men, grinning into the camera, arms looped around each other as they wore their festival shirts.

But then, Danya's was plain, and he really should find a woman who loved him to embroider it. But the thought of another woman holding Danya irritated, not that she had any right to feel that he was hers alone, but just the same—

"I've never patched or embroidered," Sidney stated suddenly.

Jessica handed her an old obviously treasured wooden hoop already fitted with fabric and a design waiting for thread. "This was Danya's grandmother's. If you have a spare moment, you might want to try it. I find that it settles me and I'm able to sort out whatever is bothering me very peacefully. Oh, here comes Ellie and Leigh and Mary Jo, just in time for tea and a few quiet moments. That means Fadey and Viktor are baby-sitting the children while they take their naps."

By the end of the hour, Sidney had learned a few embroidery stitches and she'd taken several pictures of the women sitting together, a family of women, brought together by the men they loved. She knew that when she was far away, she'd remember and treasure each one.

"Take the hoop with you," Jessica offered gently. "It's wonderful therapy. It feels like—it feels like you're sharing something with Louise."

In the Amoteh Resort's manager's suite, Sidney unfolded the hoop and the cloth and tried a few of the stitches Jessica had shown her. There was no way Sidney could fit into this family. An e-mail check revealed jobs in the Andes and Egypt, photographing new archaeological finds. A horse lover's magazine needed shots of thoroughbreds and racing, and a photographic spread was needed in an Italian cookbook. All were good paying jobs. She could take several assignments, back to back, and—

The next e-mail was from Bulldog. She answered his typical brief question "Where are you?" with "Africa. Am fine. Doing a witch doctor ceremony in the jungle shoot. The spear came out okay."

Sidney rubbed her forehead where a heavy ache had just lodged. She couldn't stay much longer and couldn't explain the tears that had begun to fall. She wiped her face roughly, ashamed that she was so emotional, and tried a few of the stitches.

Suddenly the sound on her laptop announced another incoming e-mail. It was her father. "Where exactly? Stretch and Junior are in Africa doing some beach volleyball tournament."

Sidney turned off her laptop. It was only a matter of time before her father pinned down her location and came to see "what the hell you are doing by taking these sissy assignments?"

She didn't have much time and she'd better make the most of it. Waste not, want not had always been her motto and she didn't intend to waste a moment with Danya.

Danya was just folding clothes taken from the dryer when he heard Sidney yell, "Stepanov, I know you're in there."

Evidently Sidney had discovered his secret sooner than he had planned, Danya decided as he walked to his new house's front door and opened it. He welcomed Sidney with a broad sweep of his hand.

She was wearing a bikini top, a Hawaiian-print pareo around her waist and her hiking boots. Price tags fluttered from the scanty yellow bikini top and the brightly floral pareo as she tramped into the spacious barren living room.

With her hands on her hips, she frowned and surveyed the house and Danya thought how a small woman, swaggering in that outfit could cause a man's mind to go blank.

"So this is it. The house you just bought. I was in Leigh's swimwear shop at the resort, trying on clothes and some woman—the previous owner of this house came in, chattering away about moving to Missouri. She was just winding up packing up their old house, buying some goodies for relatives, and was thrilled to make a sale of this home to a Mr. Danya Stepanov. Then some other woman—Marcella, I think— moaned over how the Stepanov men got free of her clutches and that you—"

She pushed her finger into his chest. "She said how you, Stepanov, had the look of the next one who intended to get married. So they stood there, chatting—the two women, one who had sold the house and one who thinks *that you've got marriage on your mind—with me.* And those are freshly planted rosebushes outside—probably the very same one that you harvested for that bouquet yesterday."

"So?" Danya was having trouble focusing on the problem at hand, that he didn't want anything to upset the way they were living together at the cabin. But Sidney was out of breath and flushed, and in her taut anger, her pale breasts were shimmering and soft. From the look of the price tags on her clothing, she had just hiked out the shop located within the resort, through the Amoteh's door and down the steps and across the town's streets and up over to the hill to this house. He traced the upper edge of the yellow bikini and took a slow look down Sidney's neatly curved waist, those rounded hips and the length of one leg, bared by the pareo to the boot that she was tapping on the floor, a definite sign of anger. "Nice outfit."

"I'd planned to ask you out for a date, but I've changed my mind." She tramped back to the laundry room where another load of their clothing was washing. Danya followed, appreciating the sway of her hips, the way the pareo flirted around her thighs and legs. Sidney lifted the lid of the washer and when it stopped, she reached down to peer inside.

That allowed Danya a mind-blowing view of her curved backside and little kept him from holding those hips and lifting her and—

"You're washing my clothes, dammit." Sidney fished out her jeans and turned angrily to him.

Danya's vision of entering her feminine warmth, holding those hips in his hands, bending her over and having her slid reluctantly away. "Is that a crime?"

Sidney's eyes were dark with anger as she threw the jeans on top of the washer. "I haven't asked you to baby-sit me. We're just sharing quarters, you know. I take care of myself."

Danya leaned back against the kitchen counter and crossed his arms. "You've got a chip on your shoulder, lady. And we're doing more than 'sharing quarters.' We're sharing a bed and we have steady ongoing activities in it."

She inhaled sharply, clearly struck by the outright and sharp reminder of their lovemaking. "Back out of my life, buster."

He pushed away his anger to ask grimly, "So what gives, sweetheart?"

"I told you, no one takes care of me. You were planning marriage, weren't you? All the time, I thought we were honest with each other, you were planning this."

"You make it sound like a crime. And that cabin is my family's, not mine. I want my own place. It's natural—"

"For you, maybe. Not for me. I wasn't cut out for staying in one place, planting flowers and doing housework."

His curt "Who asked you to?" slammed into her, taking away her breath.

Sidney pushed herself back together and realized that this was the first harsh emotional argument she'd ever had, one that cut more deeply than all the rest, the bare bone bloodletting kind of argument…the kind where emotions ran deep between love and hate and could flip and ruin relationships at a heartbeat. She could either back away, or she could—

Danya was already in motion, grimly picking her up and carrying her into another barren room. It was spacious and big and overlooked the ocean. "If this had a bed in it, we'd be in it now, you contrary, sexy, tormenting, half-pint, frustrating— That's the vanity I made for you there. Not exactly the way that I wanted to give it to you, but it's for you anyway. I thought I might lie in bed and watch you do the things women do."

"For me? You made it for me?" It was lovely, small and perfect, with a mirror framed in walnut and a small stool in front of the knee hole.

"There's no cushion. Women sometimes like to match the fabric-whatevers, pillows and bedspreads." Carrying her still, Danya walked through another doorway. "But on with the tour— I thought you'd like this for an office where you can do your own graphic work on your photos, and in here, there's no windows. I thought a dark room, maybe. You said that if you didn't do digital work, you wanted to develop film, and not just send it to someone to process for you."

"But—"

"You're damned irritating, sweetheart," Danya stated grimly and strode into another smaller room. "There are four more of these and a good-size playground out back. Stop squirming."

"Put me down, you big ape."

"Now those are words every man wants to hear, dear heart." Danya dropped her lightly to her feet and glared at her.

She tested the emotional static between them. Caught by the small rocker and the crib, obviously of Stepanov design,

Sidney couldn't move. This room was meant for a nursery, for children that Danya should have.

As if reading her mind and not wanting to define the furniture's real purpose in his house, Danya stated roughly, "I'm keeping them here for storage."

Chills ran up Sidney's spine. She couldn't imagine living in this house, raising children— She'd only taken care of herself and the world of things that needed to be done for an infant, a tiny little infant—

"You're white and trembling, Sidney. Just because we're 'sharing quarters' doesn't mean you're doomed into anything else."

"You're really mad, aren't you?"

"There's nothing like a woman in a romantic mood," he stated curtly, his eyes blue-gray and fierce. The lines around his mouth were tight and angry. "All sweet and receptive and—"

She hurried back to the large bedroom. The vanity was beautiful and simple and when she sat on the stool, her reflection looked back at her. She was flushed and soft and her eyes were filled with dreams. "Is this how you see me?" she asked in a whisper when Danya came to stand behind her.

His answer was unsteady. "Not always. Sometimes I see more."

His hands rested on her shoulders and Sidney lifted them in front of her, studying the large callused palms, those long capable fingers. On impulse, she kissed the center of his palm and then the other and nuzzled her face into them. "It's lovely. I've never owned a piece of furniture in my lifetime. But I can't take it."

Danya slid his hands from hers. "Whatever you want," he murmured unsteadily. "I sure don't want you to be burdened with something you don't want."

Then he walked away into the large living room and the woman in the mirror started to crumble and then to cry.

That muffled sob stopped Danya like a brick wall. He could either walk out the door, or return to face the image of

Sidney crying. The latter won and Danya held his breath as he crouched beside her.

"I never cry," she whispered unevenly between her hands. "I hate feeling drippy and soggy."

"So do I," he said in an attempt to lighten the uncertain emotional moment between them. Danya took her hands away from her face and found that her lashes were damp and spiked and her eyes shimmered with tears. Danya held both her hands in his while he gently wiped away her tears with his thumb, then he kissed her palms.

"I hate being emotional, too," Sidney admitted unevenly.

"Me, too. So are you going to ask me for that date or not?" he asked as he stood and lifted her into his arms.

When Danya sat on the stool, Sidney looked at their reflections. "You're too big to be sitting here, Stepanov. I think I'm starting to like you too much. That just complicates everything."

"How so?"

"We're having a nice time now, but eventually, you'd want more. You should have more. You'd be short-changed because I'm not geared for a permanent relationship. I'd let you down. Or hurt you, like I did just now. I'd fail you somehow. I just now decided that was why Ben suited me so, because he didn't have any big ideas before Fluffy got him. He wasn't pushy at all. You are."

"You're making decisions for the both of us, right? I'm not going to have any input?" He fought that lash of irritation; Sidney was an unusual woman and one who was terrified of relationships. Why? Because Ben had hurt her? Or was there some other reason?

Sidney frowned and pushed away to stand in front of him. "End of story," she repeated firmly as she turned to walk out of the house.

"Not quite," Danya murmured quietly as he watched her from a window. "Not quite."

Eight

Danya knew who they were immediately.

Two almost six feet tall, very fit women, wearing tank tops, fishing vests, and long, tight jeans that ended in work boots entered the Seagull's Perch where Danya was tending bar. The mid-July tourist season had added customers, and as part-owner with his brother, Danya sometimes filled in. With Sidney holed up at the Amoteh Resort for two days and avoiding him, his nights were long and endless. When he hadn't been home, she'd come back and had placed the earrings on his cabin table. He'd sat for a long time, holding those dainty garnet and gold earrings, and hurting deep inside.

Sidney's message was clear: She wanted nothing of Danya, or a life with him.

The women, both wearing very short sun-streaked hair, had Sidney's large dark eyes, were evidently older than Sidney; they wore the look of the world and of revenge and they seemed to be looking for trouble. Or for him, which was the same thing.

They moved to a side table in the shadows and one flipped a wooden chair around, straddling it, her tanned, fit arms braced across the back. The other sat, leaned her chair back against the wall, crossed her arms over her chest, and placed her boots on the table. They eyed him as Danya wiped the smooth surface of a bar imported from San Francisco's early riproaring days.

If the Blakelys had come calling, he wasn't going to refuse a showdown. He poured pitchers of free beer for the men standing at the bar, loaded a tray with three mugs and a filled beer pitcher, and walked to the women's table.

He poured the mugs full and sat at their table. Both women eyed him coldly, suspiciously, and apparently, it was up to him to make the introductions. Sidney had told him about her sisters: Stretch was an archeologist and Junior was an engineer. "Stretch and Junior, I presume?"

"Stretch," the woman straddling the chair answered.

"I'm Junior." The blonde leaning back against the wall folded her arms across her chest.

"Loverboy, I presume?" Stretch asked coolly.

"You're in trouble, bud. You hurt our little sister," Junior said.

Danya sipped his beer; he didn't like someone else pointing out the obvious—he was in trouble because every time he thought about Sidney, he wanted to haul her somewhere and set matters straight between them…or make love to her, which in the current state of affairs wouldn't solve anything.

Then, too, he resented their charge; the sisters had pegged the wrong person for the injury. Sidney wasn't exactly innocent. "Don't you think that's between us?"

"No," both women answered adamantly.

"It's a family package, loverboy," Stretch stated, watching him.

"Sid is just a kid, and she's all broken up about some joker who just pulled the same act as you. You knew she was on the rebound, Stepanov, and you did the old wine-and-dine dance with her, gave her flowers, that sort of thing…then you nailed her, right?"

Junior's evaluation was basically correct and that truth irritated. "Did she tell you that?"

"Sid is tough. She isn't saying much, but she looks like hell and she's eating candy bars. Stretch thought she was crying when she called to check in—our family has regular check-in times. Now why would she be upset?" Junior asked. "You just had to take advantage of her, didn't you? Now you've had your fun and you're done. You probably gave her the old kiss-off routine—"

Their eyes traced someone who had just come into the bar and Danya turned to see a tall older man, graying, with a hard heavily jowled face and wearing an attitude like a—

"Bulldog," Stretch's and Junior's welcomes were more like statements, as if they'd been expecting their father. Stretch's foot pushed a chair out for him.

Bulldog's six-foot-six height and three hundred pounds sat heavily and he eyed Danya. "Sid has clammed up and she's still eating chocolate bars. She's going to be sick. Is this loverboy?"

This family spent no time getting to the bare bones. "I am Danya Stepanov. You must be Sidney's father?"

Bulldog ignored Danya's extended hand. "Her name is Sid."

Danya attempted to stay pleasant. "Can I offer you a drink?"

"I'm not here for tea and crumpets, mister," Bulldog growled. "You shouldn't play light and fast with women, especially my daughter."

"I admit to the fast part. We started off too fast. But I want to marry Sidney."

Bulldog's cold silver eyes narrowed suspiciously. "That's Sid, I told you. So you're on the spot, squirming and you've come up with plan to put us off, right? Well, I guess there's one way we can find out—we'll ask Sid if you've said anything about it to her. You probably know that she's holed up, looks like hell, and she's sticking some colored thread through some material—weird looking thing. I checked you out—

you've got a lot of family around here, but that won't make any difference. They can't protect you."

He glanced at his daughters. "Now, I know my daughters are women, full-grown, but we're a family and we take care of our own. No fast-talking pretty boy is going to play easy with any one of them without having hell to pay."

Danya met Bulldog's eyes. In a blunt-talking family, it was best to speak plainly. "If I have my way, you're looking at Sid's future husband and just maybe the father of your grandchildren."

Bulldog blinked at that and seemed stunned. "My little Sid? She's little and a scrapper, but a wife and a mother? She'd be bored in no time...she's like us, ready to travel at a minute's notice—"

"I'd like your permission to marry your daughter."

"You bastard. You got her pregnant, didn't you?" Stretch demanded as she leaned forward to grip Danya's shirt in her fist.

"No, but I'd like to, if that's what Sidney wants," Danya answered honestly.

The door crashed open and the men at the bar stilled and Danya knew immediately who had entered the bar. The steady tramp of the boots approaching their table was familiar. "Hi, sweetheart—"

Sidney's slender hand reached to grip her sister's arm. "Let him go, Stretch. I thought you were all going out to dinner."

Bulldog, Stretch and Junior looked sheepish. "We were planning to order fish and chips somewhere. They're supposed to be good around here. We just stopped in for a beer—"

"The fish and chips places are closed." Sidney didn't buy their excuses and tugged Stretch's hand from Danya. Her voice was low and dangerous. "I said, 'let him go.'"

"You can't be protecting this guy, Sid," Stretch grumbled, while Danya tried to adjust to a woman defending him. Her fingers had enough pressure on Stretch's arm to indicate that Sidney meant to back up her order. He added that fact to his There's a Chance She Loves Me bin.

Sidney jerked it right out again. "He's still in love with his wife and blames himself for the car wreck that killed her. It wasn't his fault, but he's got this thing about honor and he feels that he could have avoided the wreck and didn't. They say there's a curse on this place, put there by a Hawaiian chieftain—just maybe we're both cursed. Maybe I just came by at the wrong time for us both—got it?"

That distracted Stretch, the archeologist; she released Danya, leaned forward, her long body tensed. "Sometimes there's truth in those old stories. I don't suppose there are any digs around here? Any work been done on the landscape to see if any artifacts are around, any high-aerial work?"

Danya wasn't going to be distracted from making his point with Sidney and the Blakelys. "It's true that I'll always love my wife in a special way, tucked deep inside my heart, and I'm not looking for a replacement or a substitute. I've probably picked the most contrary woman alive to fall in love with, and that would be your sister."

"Most people like me—" Sidney began hotly in her own defense.

"Sure. They just don't know you like I do."

"Ben loved her, too," Junior stated adamantly. "And look what he did to her."

"I am damn tired of hearing about Ben," Danya warned quietly and looked straight at Sidney while he continued talking, "Chief Kamakani was supposed to have been captured and enslaved by whalers, whose ship sunk in a storm off shore. He made it to land, but he never got back to the woman he loved and he placed a curse on this whole area."

That tidbit played out as he expected: Stretch's eyes narrowed; her expression resembled a hawk spotting prey. "You don't say," she murmured thoughtfully.

Danya dropped in another tidbit, just to up her interest: "Has to do with women knowing their own minds, removing the curse by dancing in front of the grave."

He met Sidney's frown, warning him not to tell where they

had first met. He smiled coldly, just to let her know that night was between them. "I go up there sometimes." If Sidney wanted to elaborate, that was her choice.

"It's just a grave up on Strawberry Hill, a bunch of rocks," Sidney answered curtly. Apparently she didn't want to explain her mistaken jumper theory. "I want you all out of here, now."

"Sid, you can't ask me to walk away from information that could lead to a good find—" Stretch began.

Facing down her tall athletic family, Sidney's body was fiercely taut, her eyes locked to them. She crossed her arms in front of her chest. "I mean it."

Danya slowly took in the way that posture made her breasts push up in the sports bra she was wearing and then he tilted his head to look down her backside, the nice curve of her bottom, the sleek line of her legs. Sidney glanced at him, blinked and suddenly blushed. "Stop that."

Bulldog did the huffing, outraged father-thing, sputtering for a moment. Stretch and Junior glared at the man who had victimized their little sister, a silent warning that when Sidney wasn't around, he was in for unhappy times. "You didn't let us take care of Ben when he ditched you to marry Fluffy, and now you're protecting this guy?"

"I'm going to go finish off Ben myself. When I'm ready, I'll take care of Danya."

"I'd like that…a nice little sweet conversation with you to clear the air." Danya smiled tightly at Sidney. "I was just asking your father's permission to marry you."

Sidney's head pivoted to him, her eyes wide. "You what?"

"You heard me."

For a moment, she was speechless, then her voice quivered with rage. "Hey, bud, *I'm* the one to ask."

With the sense that he had nothing to lose, Danya asked, "Well, will you?"

"Are you pregnant, Sid?" Bulldog asked uneasily.

"Not that I know of, sir."

Danya noted the fresh tear trails on her cheek and pride

caused him to fight drawing her down to his lap. "There's a marriage offer on the table. A long engagement would be fine with me. We'd get to know each other better, and I don't like the idea of you talking with Ben."

"Oh, you don't?" she challenged. Her smirk said that was exactly what she would do.

"How've you been, Sidney?" he asked quietly, because her fear of his marriage proposal had been easily noted earlier and Bulldog had been right: Sidney did look like she'd been going through hell.

Her dark brown eyes burned down at him; her fists clenched at her side. "What do you mean by asking Bulldog that?"

She'd made his permission-to-marry sound like an insult and Danya accepted the fact that trouble still brewed between them.

"So you love me, huh?" he asked tightly, fighting his temper as he stood. Danya signaled Sam, who had just entered the bar, that he was leaving. Sam, a full-time bartender who'd had a few hours off to attend his daughter's evening piano recital, nodded.

While Sidney fought for an answer to question about loving him, Danya reached for her and found her open lips with his own. The kiss wasn't sweet, but passionately filled with frustration and hunger.

Sidney's body tensed just for a heartbeat and then she opened herself for the kiss, her body taut against his, her arms locked around her neck. When Danya put her slightly away, her face was flushed, her eyes drowsy. He held her upper arms just that minute while she found her balance, and then he stepped back.

"That about says it, I guess," he said before turning and walking out of the bar.

Danya lay in bed at two o'clock in the morning. Three nights without Sidney curled against him was long enough, but the Blakelys had circled her protectively. Apparently, they weren't leaving her to fall victim to his evil desires. He'd have to go through them to get her.

He threw back the sheet and came to his feet; he wasn't an impulsive man, but Sidney had changed him. With her, he had to act fast, stepping up the pace. "If I have to, I have to."

A half hour later, he walked through the hushed, luxurious walls of the Amoteh Resort. There was only one way to face the Blakely bunch and that was outright, he thought grimly as he rapped on the door of the Seawind Suite.

When Bulldog opened the door, he was in an undershirt and sweat pants, cut off at the knee. He eyed Danya warily. "Yeah?"

"You like it here?" A nice conversational lead for what he wanted to say, Danya decided.

"Not really. It's too fancy-foo-foo. Is that what you want, boy? To ask about my comfort?"

"I already asked you the question that matters. I don't have your answer yet—or hers." Danya watched Sidney come to stand beside her father, Stretch and Junior loomed close by. Sidney's dark brown eyes were shimmering in tears, she looked small and wounded, and Danya wanted to hold her. He met Bulldog's scowl. "We moved too fast, but that doesn't change the feeling I have for her."

"Sid is a fast mover, boy. She usually gets what she wants," Bulldog murmured softly as he put his arm around Sidney, a father gathering his daughter close and tender. "You have to keep up. Don't feel bad if you can't. Most men can't keep up with my girls."

"I'm just finishing a few things here and then I'm leaving. I'm not marrying you," Sidney whispered unevenly.

"I'll take what I can get," Danya said and because his throat was tight with pride and emotion, he turned and walked away, out into the night.

He returned to his bed and damned himself for wanting a woman who wasn't like any other—on the other hand, that was exactly why he loved her. The wind chimes tinkled quietly, lonely on his porch and the waves broke endlessly upon the sand as he thought about how they met, up on Strawberry

Hill, and how Sidney had been mourning the loss of Ben. Now, just maybe, she was still in love with him.

At three-thirty, the cabin door opened slowly. Sidney entered, closing it behind her.

She undressed slowly and in the shadows, her curved body eased into the bed beside him. "Finish what you started," she whispered unevenly.

"There's more than this between us," Danya returned, even as he drew her into his arms and found the softness of her throat with his lips. Lying against him, she was already damp and fragrant and holding him tight, her insole rubbing his calf. She smoothed his hair, his shoulders, his back with her open hands, pressing him close, as if drawing him into her, imprinting his body into hers....

"Danya...." she whispered achingly, her lips against his jaw.

He understood the sound of goodbye, the sweetness of her kisses, soft against his, her body flowing against him. Her lips trailed to his ear, her face nuzzling his as he breathed unsteadily, holding his pride, keeping his silence.

If she needed to give him a sweet memory, he intended to return the favor, hoarding this last night for midnights to come.... His instincts told him to hold her, to possess her, and fighting his emotions, leaning over her, Danya held her wrists beside her head. "You know how I feel—that I love you?"

"Yes—"

In the shadows, her face was pale, her eyes enormous. "You feel the same, don't you?" he asked roughly, surprised that his pride could slip so, to ask what should be freely given....

The shadows were in her eyes now, a silent plea for him to understand— "It won't work, Danya—"

He couldn't wait for a denial that could tear his soul from him, but leaned down to brush his lips against hers. "Then let's make this night last—"

He tasted that smooth skin on his way down to her breasts, cradled them as she arched up onto his keeping, treated the tender peaks with lips and tongue and teeth until she left that safe, guarded place where she kept herself away from him. Her body heated, pulsing against him, and aware that Sidney could move to the ultimate pleasure too quickly, Danya held the slow pace without yielding to her trembling, her rapid, uneven breath telling him that she wanted him deep inside—

He nuzzled her belly, heard her racing heart and the hiss of her indrawn breath as her hands gripped his head. His blood pounded and his body hurt, demanding release, but Danya strained to keep his course, to make Sidney remember this night, remember him....

To his touch, she was hot and moist and the incredible sounds that came, strained and uneven from her, told him that one touch could take her flying—

Too soon, he thought, rising to kiss her, to slant his open mouth to hers, to let her suckle his tongue, whimpering, her hips rising against his hand. Then she pushed him inches away, rising over him. Her fingers locked with his, her body pushing down, damp and waiting, rocking upon him.

Danya turned suddenly, fighting the primitive need to take her, to slide within her. He ran his hands over her body, cupping her bottom, then turned her stomach down on the bed, bracing himself over her, resting intimately against her feminine damp softness. He nuzzled her face, smoothed the dampness with his cheek, slid his hand around to her belly and lower, cupping her, moving, slowly rhythmically with her, though they were still separate, kissing her taut shoulders, her nape, her cheek....

If she was his curse, a woman he could never forget, and never have, he would take this time at his leisure, take everything, demand everything—

He moved slowly, fearing that the storm would come too soon, turning her and then her eager hand slid to find him and he held his breath, forcing himself still— In their lovemaking, she had never gone so far, cradling him, gloving him....

Danya cradled her face with his hands, feeding upon the

taste of her mouth, letting the rhythm of tongue and bodies flow more quickly. Heat flew, whirled around them, binding them tighter until nothing existed but her—

He heard that quiet, keening cry of her pleasure in the distance, above the pounding of his heart, above the heat claiming him—

Because he couldn't let her go, leave him just yet, Danya held her tightly, resting momentarily, before demanding even more—

This time, Sidney surprised him as she moved sleekly over him, rocking, demanding, primitive—perfect....

She left him in the dawn, with the wind chimes gently singing, the waves breaking upon the sandy beach.

Danya watched the mist enfold her and knew he'd carry the taste of her forever, that no other woman could fill his heart, that he'd remember forever the night that had passed.

Was it his curse? he asked, mocking himself, to love such a woman, a woman who feared and fought what ran so strong and fiercely between them?

Danya smiled tightly and watched the two tall athletic women stride up the pathway to his new house. Only hours after Sidney had walked off into the mist—hell, she was almost running, terrified of being shackled into marriage or anything else with him—he'd expected the Blakely family.

He turned off the table saw he'd been using to make a railing for the wooden deck of his new house. He'd been wondering if he could actually live in a house hollow with dreams of a lover, who was now in flight. "Hello, ladies," he said pleasantly.

"Sid is gone, loverboy, and there's no one to protect you now," Junior warningly said as she and Stretch stepped up to the wooden deck.

Stretch popped her knuckles and widened her stance as if preparing for a fight. "Our baby sister is a pitiful, sobbing wreck. You need a lesson in turning on the charm and hurting women, loverboy."

"Do you know where she went?" He tried not to appear too

interested, because the Blakelys probably knew and would hoard that information from him—the "Loverboy."

"Flew out of here as fast as her rental car would take her. Sid has assignments all over the world. She'll check in when she's good and ready. But don't hold your breath that she'll contact you. We don't buy that 'rebound' story, that you loved your wife and Sid just came into your life at the wrong time and you made a play for her."

Junior was studying the house. "You're on the same level as Ben."

"And you're pretty irritating yourself, Junior," Danya stated pleasantly, although he could understand their appraisal— Sidney had put him in the Ben-bin, sex as needed, come and go freely, and that irritated. Danya had admitted his love and she'd walked away from what they could have—and he wasn't feeling sweet about that….

He had to admire the Blakely family, because they protected their own, just as the Stepanovs would do. The dynamics were very different, but the Blakelys' love was strong. If he had to love a hardheaded woman, he might as well get to know Sidney's family better—if possible. "Had your breakfast yet this morning?"

"No, why? Delaying the inevitable, loverboy?"

If Sidney's sisters were anything like her, they were healthy eaters and feeding them might trim their need for revenge. And just maybe, he might pick up some tidbits about Sidney. "Just offering a little friendly bacon and eggs and hash browns—maybe some toast and juice? I just stocked the refrigerator and haven't tried out this new stove yet."

"Don't tell me you cook for Sid?" Junior asked warily as she leaned to one side, looking around him into the house.

"I never asked her to take care of me. That wasn't what our relationship was about."

"Yeah, you just wanted sex, right? And you picked on Sid when she was vulnerable. We should have kicked Ben's butt and we may still—right after we're finished with you."

"Give Ben a break, will you? He's an expectant father now."

Stretch and Junior shared an uneasy look. "I can't hurt a guy who's expecting," Junior said and Stretch nodded in agreement.

Danya thought of Sidney's equal hunger for him and decided against adding fuel to the Blakelys' already established dislike of him. He shrugged lightly. "An architect designed this house. Take a look around if you want. I'll start breakfast."

Stretch was standing, long legs braced studying the view of the ocean and the peninsula called Strawberry Hill. "How do I get up there? That's where the grave is, isn't it?"

"Uh-huh. Years ago, someone discovered what they thought was an artifact up there, maybe a war club resembling something Kamakani might have used. Where's Bulldog?"

"Where's that club now? I'd like to verify the style.... Bulldog is talking to your father. He figures that's his role since his baby girl has been seduced by you. He didn't buy the marriage offer, because he knew you were on the spot and trying to slime out of it. Besides that, Sid would never settle down permanently. Who in this town keeps historical records?"

"Try the local soap shop. Ask for Willow."

Danya noted Junior's tall, lithe body prowling in the house behind him; she was exploring the hidden panels of the entertainment center. If he could keep both women interested long enough, they just might stay and that might mean Sidney would come looking for her family. "Let me start breakfast and then we can talk. My laptop is set up in the other room, an office, if you want to research anything— Well, okay, then," Danya added softly as Stretch moved by him, into the house. Junior pointed her sister to a hallway and Stretch hurried out of sight.

One thing about the Blakely sisters, they wasted no time in getting what they wanted.

Danya just hoped that Sidney wanted him and he had plenty of patience....

* * *

In her New York brownstone apartment three days later, Sidney studied the duplicate pictures she'd taken of the Stepanov family, the Stepanov Furniture, and the Amoteh Resort. Her finger traced the pictures of the Amoteh Resort's Tea Room, the gorgeous soft lighting, the delicate cups and saucers beside Mary Jo's raspberry filled cookies. The gorgeous *samovar* sat near the traditional glasses with elegant metal holders.

The dish of strawberries had had to be rearranged after Danya had removed one, feeding it to her and she had returned the intimate gesture. She had loved hand feeding Danya, watching his darkening, intent expression as he accepted the strawberry; it had been as if the world had slowed, heartbeats hours apart, rather than seconds.

On impulse, she picked up the telephone and dialed Mikhail's private office number. His voice was brisk, businesslike. "Mikhail."

"This is Sid. I'm doing a follow-up, no other reason to call. Just wanted to check to see if you were satisfied with the takes for the brochure. I guarantee my work, you know. I don't want dissatisfied customers, not good for the reputation. Oh, and make certain that you supply my photographer's permission for the printers."

On the other end of the line, Mikhail was too quiet. Then he said, "Everything is fine, Sid. Thanks. You're welcome here any time, you know."

Because she hadn't heard from her family, Sidney asked tentatively, "I suppose my family checked out?"

"Yes, just after you left."

"Um…did they say anything about where they were going?"

"Not to me." There was someone else she could ask, but she wouldn't. "Okay, thanks. I guess they're traveling, sometimes it's a couple of weeks before I hear from them."

"Anything else, Sid?"

"Um." *Have you seen Danya? Is he okay? Has he said anything about me?* "Um, no, nothing. Thanks. Bye."

Sidney hugged a couch throw pillow. *Danya....*

She wouldn't be good for him. She wasn't the stay-in-one-place, little housewifey kind.... He'd hate her in the end.... There was no way she could fit into his life.... He deserved a woman who— "I love you," he'd said.

Sidney jackknifed into sitting position and rummaged through the glossy pictures on her coffee table to find one of Danya, the salty breeze taking his hair back from that rugged face, those sky-blue eyes narrowed against the sun, that devastating grin into the camera when she'd surprised him.

The entire Stepanov family portrait lay next to Danya's photograph and she'd smoothed the others away. Taken in front of Fadey's huge fireplace, the family was large and proud. As she studied them, one by one, Sidney whispered the names of the babies, parents, proud grandparents, husbands and wives—

Leaning slightly against Alexi, Jessica cradled Danika Louise. Mikhail held his stepdaughter close to his side, Mary Jo held hands with Fadey, who sat next to Viktor. Then men wore their festival shirts, loose with wide collars, embroidered — But Danya's was plain....

Sidney had left his grandmother's embroidery hoop in Mikhail's office, fearing that something so cherished could be lost in the mail. And it was best that some other woman complete his life....

Danya.... Safe, big, strong, masculine...close, sensual, hot, hungry...fierce lover, taking, giving...tender friend, sharing....

Flipside: Brooding, arrogant, traditional, a family man if ever there was one. Worse—he cooked and cleaned and washed her clothing and seemed content that she had no housekeeping skills whatsoever.

The whole tall, muscular, good-looking package was irritating, unsuitable for the lifestyle that she had wanted.... "I love you," he'd said.

Just maybe she'd been on the rebound from Ben and had gotten blindsided by Danya, who despite what he said about tucking Jeannie deep within his heart, was still in love with his wife.

Who was he anyway?

But she knew: Danya was a part of her now, a man who had shared her body, making love, not sex to her. Now that was scary—lovemaking was more than sex, and now no-thanks to Danya, she knew the difference. It would probably haunt her forever. *She hadn't heard from him. Was he all right?*

A quick sly call to Mary Jo said that she loved the photographs for the furniture shop and that the brochure she was creating was coming along nicely. "Come back to see us, dear," Mary Jo invited in her soft Texas drawl.

Sidney replaced the telephone. Danya's aunt hadn't said a thing about him....

But more importantly, because Sidney had always known her own mind and was now questioning her next assignment from an assortment, trying to balance her life and needs without Danya, now that she'd had a taste of him— "Who am I?"

Sidney lurched to her feet and started pacing. "Okay, so everything happened so fast. It usually does with me. I know what I want and I go for it. I went for Danya. He seemed like a nice guy—okay, he is a nice guy—but he comes with all sorts of problems. The best thing for us both is just to walk off and forget the whole thing."

But could she?

Not one to waste time, Sidney hurried out of her apartment with two things on her mind: One to find the nearest stitchery shop, and two, to finish off Ben. She'd loved him forever, and she'd been deeply hurt and angry when she'd met Danya.

It all started on Strawberry Hill.... "He wasn't going to jump off that cliff. He loved his wife, but he also loved his family and life...."

Anytime there was a clog in her thinking, in choosing a direction, it was best to start at the root of the problem and work to the resolve.

And where was her family, anyway?

Did Danya miss her? Was he thinking about her?

He'd created a real hole in her life and marred her thinking. She had to deal with him, and herself. Hurrying now, she opened a craft and hobby store door, walked into the cluttered interior and felt fear rise up her spine. The shop held everything that was unnatural to her—ribbons, cloth, needles, patterns.... She hated fear, she really did, and worse she hated failure. But because of Danya, she was experiencing both.

When the clerk came to help her, Sidney wasted no time in getting what she wanted, just as she had Danya. "Fix me up with some flowery embroidery stuff, okay? Threads, easy design, maybe some how-to book, needles, hoop, whatever."

Back in her apartment, Sidney made quick travel arrangements. Now all she had to do was to finish off Ben, and no longer on the rebound, she could untangle her feelings about Danya and thus finish him off, too....

Sidney had the uneasy sense that she just might not be able to complete that mission.

She glanced at her e-mail, hoping for Danya's name, and nothing appeared. Her message machine, which she usually managed by remote contained the same number of messages as when she had last checked. Sidney flipped open a picture book in which she had stored the flattened remains of the beautiful orchid corsage he'd given her and fought tears.

"That's all he's good for, making me cry." Well, her body admitted as she hugged a pillow close to her, Danya was good for other things.

Danya....

On Strawberry Hill, Danya lifted his face to the fierce wind and rain striking him. He'd met Sidney, the reason for his sleepless, aching nights, on this same high cliff a month ago. It was now mid-July and she was in his every thought.

He could go after her.

He could e-mail or send flowers or call.

But he wouldn't. He wasn't feeling exactly tender toward Sidney. She didn't trust him. Another man had hurt her and Sidney wasn't taking chances again.

None of the above equated to love.

He bent quickly and grabbed a tuft of grass, lifting and freeing it to the fierce salt-scented wind. Wherever she was, he wanted her to think about him, to ache for him.

Uncomfortable with constant anger and the need to tear Sidney away from him—or go after her—Danya turned to Chief Kamakani's grave. "Don't wait for Sidney to come dancing in front of your grave. She's a curse in herself and she's probably still grieving over Ben…. Does she love me? That irritating little fast-moving, argumentative, tough-mouthed scrap of female? I think so, or maybe, on some level, I'm just as perverse as she is. On the rebound? Not a chance, at least for me. Sidney will have to make up her own mind about her next move—but I don't plan to make it easy for her. So you see, Chief, your curse is pretty effective…."

He'd given Sidney his heart and his dreams and she'd walked out of his life….

But he had one thing she wouldn't walk away from—her family, living in his house.

She'd come back for them, and when she did, she'd have to reckon with Danya and what brewed between them….

Nine

Sidney rammed her rental pickup into low gear, preparing for the highway grade that descended into Amoteh. In the two weeks since she'd left the oceanside town, Bulldog hadn't returned to his condominium in Maine; none of his friends there had seen him, and he wasn't in his usual worldwide haunts. Stretch and Junior and Bulldog were answering her e-mail, but had avoided pinpointing their actual location. As world travelers, they could be anywhere.

In the space of a week, while Sidney had gone to Ben's Wisconsin farm and picked up an assignment shooting cornfields and cattle, she'd lost her entire family. By the second week, after shooting a sailing regatta in Boston, she was really worried.

But everything seemed the same in Amoteh. The Amoteh Resort jutted out into the midmorning sunlight from the pines surrounding it. The towering totem poles of grotesque Native American masks stood near the resort. Clusters of golfers were walking on the lush green, sprawling golf course.

In late July, the Pacific Ocean lay ahead, seeming to blend into the clear blue sky. Sailboats skimmed the waves, tourist boats of all kinds bobbed beside the piers to which they were tethered. The large pier jutting out from the shoreline was lined with shops, colorful flags flying above the tourists milling below.

Sidney noted Mikhail's black BMW in the Amoteh's parking lot and drove her pickup to park nearby. She entered the Amoteh, and braced herself for the sight of Danya.

Danya had been put on the spot by her father and sisters, otherwise he never would have mentioned marriage. He was an old-fashioned guy, bound by honor; he would do the expected.

However, his delivery of marriage—"Well, will you?"—wasn't exactly romantic, and he'd seemed to be romantic earlier. But then, her family, united and defensive, could leave tulips wilted in their wake.

Sidney met Jarek in the hallway near the Stepanov Furniture Display Room; he was carrying a cardboard box. The Stepanov males were gorgeous, she decided as she walked toward him. Just the sight of a Stepanov male, so like Danya, brought that funny little squeeze around her heart—*Danya....*

"Hey, Sid," Jarek greeted her.

"Hey, Jarek."

"Open the door for me, will you? This is a box of Mom's lemon-and-beeswax polish. We're starting to market it, and I'm setting up a display inside. She may want you to do some shots of it for a separate sales brochure. Your last ones for our furniture turned out really good."

"Thanks. It's new stuff for me. I wasn't too certain how they'd turn out." Sidney followed Jarek inside; she wouldn't ask about Danya. "So how's the family, Jarek?"

While Jarek unloaded the bottles from the box, Sidney tried not to look at the bed in which she and Danya had made love that first time— She ran her hand over the smooth dark wood of a sturdy armoire and onto the blue woven mat covering a chest of drawers. He'd been so—tender and fierce.... How could she ever forget that?

She thought about the little vanity he'd given her, her first handcrafted gift from a man. Danya had been first in many ways, but she couldn't take that perfect little piece away from Amoteh. It belonged somewhere safe, where it could be tended—maybe by some woman who suited Danya better, someone who knew about polishing furniture and who would brush her hair nightly in front of the mirror. Sidney frowned when she remembered how Danya had said he'd wanted to watch from the bed—another woman and Danya in the same bedroom wasn't an image she liked.

Mary Jo entered the display room with a tray filled with a beautiful teapot and cups and saucers decorated by the Amoteh's strawberry design. "Hi, Sid. It's so nice to see you. I thought I'd have some tea while I polish the furniture. We're just starting to market my own recipe for polish and I'm pretty excited. It's my mother's recipe and I've used it for years," she said in her soft Texas drawl as she placed the tray on a small table.

Sidney studied the neatly arranged bottles. "The packaging looks great."

"Thank you, Jarek," Mary Jo said quietly and looked at her son, a silent message that she wanted to be alone with Sidney.

"Uh—okay, I have to get back to the shop. See you later," he said.

"There's nothing like having a midmorning cup of tea after polishing furniture. Just sitting and relaxing with the smell of lemon and the sense of a job well done." Mary Jo slid open a dresser drawer and removed a cloth, which she saturated with the polish. She began polishing a long dining room table and smiled at Sid. "Of course, I could polish later. Would you like to have a cup of tea with me now, Sid?"

"Oh, I couldn't—unless you'd let me help you." Just maybe, while they were working, Mary Jo might tell her about Danya.

"That would be so nice. Thank you."

Sidney hadn't polished furniture before, and she found that she enjoyed it immensely. She wondered if anyone had polished her little vanity—in the bedroom where Danya had shown her—in the bedroom where a bed would be and he just might be sharing it with some other woman. *Some other woman could be kissing Danya even now....*

And that would be perfect, she tried desperately to make herself believe, because she didn't fit into his life.

When they had finished polishing, Mary Jo served tea, and Sidney sat, surprised that she had also enjoyed the light work and the lemony scent, as Mary Jo, a proud grandmother talked about her family. Strange, Sidney thought, the softness she felt, the gentling inside as she sat with the older woman. Mary Jo's inner calmness was catching, Sidney decided, and realized how very few times she had visited quietly with women—heart-to-heart talks with her sisters didn't really qualify. Stretch and Junior had little time for deep introspection, exploring their emotions.

"Mary Jo, I was wondering if you'd happen to know where my family is—Bulldog, Stretch and Junior? I mean, they left here just after I did and though I'm on e-mail with them, I can't seem to pinpoint their location."

Mary Jo sipped her tea slowly before answering thoughtfully, "Why, I believe Bulldog is with Fadey and Viktor on the beach, baby-sitting the children."

Sidney almost spilled her tea. Her father had always meticulously avoided contact with children. "What? My father? You mean, he's here? Baby-sitting?"

"They were fishing this morning—Fadey, Viktor and Roy—"

"Roy? My dad?"

"That's his name, isn't it? Roy Blakely?"

Sidney shook her head to clear it. "I guess so. I haven't heard anyone use it before. What about Stretch and Junior?"

"I think they're on the beach, too, darlin'. Playing volleyball, I believe."

An hour later, after Sidney had greeted her missing family, she sat on a driftwood log and watched her sisters play volleyball in the sand. Their opponents on the other side of the net were two tall powerful males—Stepanov cousins, Sergei and Kiril, who were temporarily staying in the beach cabin. Stretch and Junior were strong, agile, powerful and competitive—but the men were easily beating them and the sisters were irritated.

When Sidney was first greeted by them, there was something uneasy about her family; they'd said they were taking an unexpected vacation and hadn't had time to contact her. Usually in transit, from one job and location to another, the sisters had always been vocal about job problems, insect bites, or the excitement in their work; but now they weren't talking about their next projects, only the game in progress, one they were losing badly. Bulldog stuck to basics, giving no explanation of why he hadn't contacted her. Her family had avoided telling her that they had stayed in Amoteh. Why?

Because they knew she wouldn't approve?

On the sandy volleyball court, Stretch and Junior were clearly frustrated as they lost points. Apparently, the wager was that the losers would cook dinner for the winners; the menu was the winners' choice.

Bulldog was talking with Fadey and Viktor as they sat on another log, children playing in the sand at their feet. Her father looked soft and mellow, unlike his usual brisk and tough self. He shared the grandfather look with Fadey and Viktor and was taking great interest in the construction of a sand castle near him, scooping sand into small plastic buckets for the children to use.

Without looking, Sidney recognized the long jeaned legs of the man who came to sit beside her. She tried to ignore the iced snow cone Danya held out to her, but because things were so gloomy and everyone was so happy, she sighed and took it from him. It was strawberry flavored and she sucked it, taking her time before she spoke, "You did this, didn't you?"

A sidelong glance told her that Danya looked delicious in a T-shirt and jeans, and he smelled fantastic— He sucked his snow cone, reminding her of how that mouth had treated her breasts. Beneath her chambray shirt and her tight sports bra, they ached slightly and deep inside her, her muscles clenched—

"What did I do? Too bad—Stretch just missed that serve." Danya was watching the game in progress—the ordinarily cool and dexterous Stretch had just stamped the ground and Junior was chastising her for a wrong move. The sisters usually played methodically, perfectly, and they didn't like losing.

Sidney sighed and took a bit of the crushed ice, rolling it on her tongue before swallowing. "They didn't want me to know where they were. So here they are. My family never stays long in one place and—"

The game had ended, but Danya didn't turn to Sidney. "Good game. Your sisters are good. You smell like a lemon."

"Uh-huh. I don't like this, Danya...what you've done to my family."

He licked his snow cone, tipped it a little to drink the melted ice and flavoring, and took his time responding. "I didn't do anything."

"Don't deny that you had a hand in this. Those guys—your cousins—are ringers, if I ever saw one. What do they do for a living, anyway?"

Danya shrugged easily. "Sergei races a bit. Kiril rides in rodeos."

"Oh, boy. You pulled out the competitive ones. Just how many cousins do you have?"

"Never counted. All my uncles immigrated at the same time as my father.... So how is Ben?" he asked easily.

"Happy. It's disgusting. Duck poo everywhere. He really loves Fluffy."

"That's too bad. You'll miss him."

Sidney looked at Danya, but found nothing in his expression as he watched the new game in progress—Junior had just thrown the ball into the sand, furious with Stretch for not diving for the ball. Expert players, tanned, long and lithe and dressed in sports bras and cutoffs, the sisters were rarely upset with each other's ability, but now, with taunts from the men, their irritation was obvious.

Her sisters would have to fend for themselves; Sidney had her own problem, sitting beside her, and he wasn't friendly. "I'm glad for him, I guess. We really were friends."

"Mmm. That's kind of you."

She studied him again—then Danya turned slowly to look straight at her and his blue eyes were brilliant with anger. Then she knew— "You did this deliberately, didn't you? Invite your cousins here to sidetrack my sisters? You did it to get back at me, didn't you?" she asked uneasily.

"Do you ever play volleyball with your sisters?" he asked tightly.

"You know I'm too short to compete with them. Poker is usually our game of choice, or pool. What's it to you?" She understood immediately then that he wasn't going to make friendship easy for her as Ben had.

Danya had always seemed so gentle, so thoughtful, but his smile now was cold…and he avoided her direct question about revenge. "I was just thinking that you don't seem to be the kind to stick around for a rematch. So, how have you been, Sid?"

Sid. No lover-talk, no "sweetheart," no "my darling," no little tantalizing kisses from those hard strawberry-red lips. A little frightening tingle shimmied up her nape. She hadn't seen this side of him, the cold, vengeful lover. She could admit that she'd thought of Danya almost every second—and thought of how their lives would be miserable if they married.

Then one of the Stepanov cousins hooted as his serve scored, hitting in bounds, and missed by Stretch, who was lying belly-down on the sand. She jackknifed to her feet, glared at Junior, and placed her hands on her waist. "Rematch?" she shouted hopefully.

"Not a chance. You're cooking. Steaks and baked potatoes.

Make a pie, too. And make it romantic, will you? Candles, that kind of stuff at the cabin?" Kiril returned.

"Sure, we'll take that rematch," Sergei called. "You win, we'll cook. We win, you cook *and* wear something romantic…girly-date clothes, that sort of stuff."

Stretch looked at Junior who nodded. "Agreed," Junior said grimly.

Sidney studied Sergei and Kiril. They were gorgeous and challenging and according to her father, "Roy," both were single. Apparently Bulldog had been smitten by the happy family image—and the little girl sitting on his lap, giving him a taste of her cookie. Bulldog seemed to be thoroughly enjoying himself. The picture of her family was flipping into an unfamiliar, scary scene. "This whole setup was just purely evil of you, Danya. Oh, my gosh—"

She watched spellbound as Stretch and Junior dipped under the volleyball net and kissed Kiril and Sergei respectively. They weren't sweet kisses, rather hard, forceful ones that were resentfully given without touching the men. When the kisses ended, the Stepanov males grinned. "Next time, put your arms around me," Kiril called, taunting Stretch. "Dare you."

On her way back the net, Stretch turned to scowl at him. Her return was a dark curse.

Sidney couldn't take any more of her sisters' humiliation or Danya's unexpected cold, hard side. "I'm leaving. Where's my family staying?"

Danya stood slowly, towering over her. He took her empty snow cone paper and crushed it in his fist, tossing the papers into a nearby trash barrel. "You're right. You are short."

His eyes slid coolly down her body and Sidney fought that trembling inside, the need to reach for him. Then those eyes locked with hers. "You look like hell, Sid. You look pale and tired—dreaming about Ben, were you?"

Dreaming about you….

She wanted him to hold her and—she'd never seen Danya

so cold and angry before. With someone else, she could have walked away—but then, she'd hurt him and didn't know how to say the right words. "Just tell me where they're staying and tell them that I'll be there."

"My place," Danya said slowly. "They're staying at my house."

Danya watched that information register in Sidney's wide brown eyes and damned his need for revenge. But it was there, simmering, the need to make her pay for walking away from a future they could have…. There wouldn't be another love for him, not with the damage Sidney had done to his heart—it wouldn't be fair to another woman to gift her with that dark residue of love gone wrong….

Taking it a notch deeper, he wouldn't have children with another woman and that's just how it was for him, and he knew it deep inside.

Her hair had grown just a bit, enough to catch the breeze and lift over her pretty little ears—he really liked those ears. Sidney's mouth was just as soft and pink, parted in surprise, and he remembered how sweet she tasted inside, how she'd suckled his tongue as they made love….

He continued his survey of her, taking his time to let her know that he remembered every intimacy, how she tasted, and her hunger for him. Maybe that wasn't nice, but he wasn't feeling exactly sweet. She'd knotted her chambray shirt just below her breasts, and just a bit of her sports bra showed. From there, her stomach was smooth and soft, and those jean cutoffs sagged low enough on her hips to reveal—nothing.

Now that was mind-blowing, because Danya knew exactly what those shorts concealed, all soft and fragrant— He tried to keep his focus as he continued deliberately taking in those long slender legs, down to her little bare feet braced apart in the sand. He wanted to emphasize that they'd been lovers. Then he forced his gaze upward to her face, to the hot blush riding it.

"You want to have this out here, or in private?" he asked

and damned himself again as the tears welled to her eyes and she dashed them away.

"I'm crying an awful lot now, and you're the reason. You're wrecking everything." She sat quickly, brushed her feet free of sand, and jerked on her boots.

What was he supposed to do? Forget that she'd walked out on what they could have? That she'd gone to see another man? "Oh, am I? How so? And by the way, you forgot your socks."

He scooped them from the log and Sidney swept them from him. "You planned this whole thing. You involved my family to deliberately make me come back. You kept them here."

"I wanted to know them better. Let's have this out in private." Danya bent to pick her up in his arms and started walking up the beach toward his new house. For once she wasn't arguing, but her slight sniff and the damp tears on his shoulder were telling him that something other than temper ruled her now. And he still wanted her….

When she began to squirm, he fairly dumped her to her feet, then gripped her hand as he continued walking. "I'm not going to hurt you."

She dug her boots into the sand, and Danya took a steadying breath, cursed his lack of patience—she had done that to him, wrung every bit of patience from him.

"I'm not good at this emotional stuff, guy, and you're putting me through an awful lot of it."

"Yeah, well, I haven't even started yet." And another thing—he'd never really liked to argue, either. He still didn't, but out of necessity, there was one woman in his life who really deserved a good argument from him, and he was going to give it to her.

"How dare you capture my family!"

Now, he'd really enjoyed that. And the knowledge that eventually, Sidney would come hunting them, the woman who had caused him to lose his temper, his patience and could cause him to argue. "They seem to like it. Roy is enjoying himself. You must really bully them, or else they would have told you where they were."

"I never— Okay, sometimes I have to keep them from running over me, because I'm the youngest. My dad's name is Bulldog, and you shouldn't pick on an old man.... I—"

She was staring at him and in that instant, Danya felt the air between them still, then heat slowly and swirl, binding him to her. Oh, no, he thought helplessly, as he picked up the pace. He wasn't getting all caught up in his passion for her, for the tenderness she could wrap around his heart—not this time, not without settling what brewed between them. He couldn't let her take even more of his pride—"nailing" him on the spot without some kind of admission that she really did love him—

"Where are we going?"

He wasn't going to let her take him so quickly this time, Danya promised himself firmly, not before they had settled that he loved her and he'd asked her to marry him, and she'd walked out after giving him a whole lot of herself in every way.... He'd awakened during the nights since then, dreaming about her welcoming body, that tight moist pulse of her, the sweet way she'd given herself to him—several times. No woman should ever make love to a man like that, then walk off and leave him, he decided darkly. "Someplace private to talk."

"There's plenty of beach right here."

Danya glanced at the tall beach grass that could provide privacy for lovemaking. "I don't think so. If you're going to yell at me, the wind would carry it. It just could speed up the game your sisters are already losing."

"Fine, then."

"Fine."

At his house, Sidney steamed up the steps leading from the beach. In her wake, Danya was left to admire the sway of her bottom, the long, slender strength of her legs. On his deck now, a wooden expanse with a view of Strawberry Hill from huge lawn chairs, she noted the checkerboard on the table between them. Sidney paused at the doorway leading into the house and stared at the newly installed hot tub.

"What's that? That wasn't here last time."

"Things change. Or most things do," he added curtly. The hot tub overlooking the ocean and Amoteh was where he'd treated his abused muscles after trying to work Sidney out of his system, the need to go after her…where he'd sat for two weeks and brooded about her and listened for the call she should have made…. Danya opened the sliding door for her, gesturing her inside with that gallant sweep of his hand—

His hand hesitated in mid air just above that delectable curved bottom and just then, inside his home, Sidney pivoted to him. She glanced at his open hand and at his expression, and backed away. "You wouldn't dare. Don't you dare."

"Do what?" he asked with a touch of the nastiness he felt as he took a step toward her and once inside, slid the door closed behind him. Since Sidney was backing up, he decided he might as well press his advantage—he moved toward her and watched her eyes widen as she backed away a few more feet.

"Never mind. I thought for a minute you were—"

"Going to spank you? Never crossed my mind, Sid," he stated honestly. He didn't like the dark primitive urge within him to take her now, to wipe away any other man, to let her know that she was a part of him now. New to jealousy, Danya didn't like how he was feeling. Great, just great…offer a woman a home and love and she runs to a former lover.

"Um…okay then." She continued backing nervously away from him into the center of the living room. "Who plays checkers? I saw the board outside."

"Roy does. He likes to sit in the evening and play checkers. Sometimes Fadey or my father comes over and they like to watch the sun go down together. Some of the boys Roy has met on the beach like to come over, too. Leigh's younger brother, Ryan, has a crush on your sisters—he can't make up his mind which one—but he's here a lot, talking about surfing—which apparently they like, too."

"I imagine your cousins know how to surf, too?"

Danya smiled at that. Sergei and Kiril frequently took breaks from their Montana ranch and had won a few amateur trophies in Hawaii and Australia. "A little."

Sidney was furious now, turning on him. "You can't set up my family like this, Danya, just to get at me."

"I just told them that they were welcome here. They seemed to like it. I've got plenty of room, you know." He thought of Sidney in that big bed in his bedroom, of how much he wanted her there, snuggled close to him.

Or here. Or with him, in any way she wanted him.

Her next question startled him. "So where do I bunk?"

With me. At least you need me there and there's no denying that... Instead Danya said, "Anywhere you want."

In bed, they were compatible—it was the other times that Danya intended to smooth out—but pride demanded that Sidney meet him halfway....

Sidney noted the new pool table standing alongside one wall, the cue sticks standing in the rack nearby. She studied the new living room furniture, heavy dark wood with subtle melon and brown fabric cushions. Two large Stepanov-styled chairs with cushions and footstools sat in front of the panel with the big screen television, a checkerboard table sat between them. She sniffed delicately, then trailed her hand over the new pool table on her way into the kitchen where Danya was cooking the family's pot roast dinner in his slow cooker.

When she came out, Danya said, "You're welcome to stay for dinner, if you want."

Sidney looked as if she hadn't eaten a decent meal; she looked terrified, as if her world was slipping away and she was all alone and vulnerable. He wouldn't beg— *Stay. Work this out. I know you're scared and doubting, but just give us a chance...and don't run away again, or this time, I just might come after you....*

Danya wiped the Seagull Perch's gleaming bar. At ten o'clock in the evening, he'd given Sam, the bartender, the rest of the night off. Throughout dinner, the Blakelys had been too quiet; the sisters and Bulldog had seemed uneasy. Sidney wasn't making things easy, sending dark accusing looks as she ate at the table with them. Deciding that the whole family could vent much easier without his presence, Danya had excused himself to let the Blakelys' tense, brewing argument ripen fully.

Clearly, Sidney considered them to be deserters: "You should have let me know where you were at—if you just had to stay here. Touch-points, remember? One of the Blakely family rules? Everybody knows where everybody else is?" she'd demanded darkly.

Clearly the sisters weren't relenting and after losing the volleyball games with Sergei and Kiril, they were feeling nasty: "Lay off, Sid. Bulldog likes it here, the whole baby and kid thing. We couldn't just desert him…he'd be all alone. He needed our support, because we're team players. And baby-sitting isn't that bad."

Sidney had done that blinking, take-two thing she did when she was stunned. "Huh? You baby-sit?"

"Danya does. If a man does it, why can't we? And by the way, sister dear, in order to get you by himself, he promised his cousins that he'd baby-sit for a week if they'd keep their wives from moving in on you."

Sidney had turned to Danya. "You did that?"

"Hey, I like to baby-sit," he'd said, defending himself.

"So you planned even that—"

He'd left at that point and Bulldog had followed him out onto the deck. "This could get nasty," Bulldog stated uneasily. "Think I'll just go over to Fadey and Mary Jo's and see if I can rummage up a checker game. I'd advise you to go somewhere safe since Sidney's on the warpath. She's a scrappy little thing, like her mother, and can hold her own against both Stretch and Junior if it comes to that. Better let my girls settle their own hash."

Danya placed the glasses he'd just washed onto the Seagull Perch's bar just as the door opened and Sidney entered. Her eyes locked instantly, defiantly with Danya's. Every man in the bar turned to watch her.

But then, any man would notice a curvy woman wearing a black spandex sports bra and snug black tights and worn work boots. The men who looked too long met Sidney's fierce What Are You Looking At, Bozo? glare.

She walked to the pool table, chalked up a cue stick, and began shooting. When she took her shots, bending over the table, the tight sports bra did little but enhance the swell of her breasts and men stared at that soft rounded backside, the sleek feminine legs below it.

Every man in the place stared at that soft bottom as she bent over the table and the women with them were irritated at the distraction.

Danya remembered that she hadn't worn any underclothing at the social—

"Bar is closed," he announced loudly as he whipped the bar towel over his shoulder and walked to the door, opening it. "Everyone out."

Sidney continued to shoot expertly, smoothly, ignoring the people who were grumbling and emptying the bar.

Danya closed the door and came to lean against the wall, watching her shoot pool. Over her shoulder, Sidney said, "I thought I'd walk you home."

Danya took in the curved line of her body as she lined up a shot, legs braced, elbow up as her hand gripped the cue stick, other arm extended, finger hooked to form a bridge around the stick, hand flattened to the pool tables green cloth. "Nice getup."

"Thanks. My usual when playing seriously—nothing to get in the way."

"You smell like lemon."

"Polished the vanity in your room. That beeswax-and-lemon stuff of Mary Jo's is really good. While we were at it, Stretch and Junior and I polished all the furniture in the house. Odd house—the walls are totally bare, not that much furniture either."

"You came here to tell me I need a decorator?"

"No, I came to tell you that your cousins have got my sisters in a snit. They hate losing. I just hope you're enjoying it."

Bulldog had been right—when the sisters got into an argument, it was better to hole up, away from the flurry. "So how did that go? Your sisters and you?"

"We worked out a few kinks." She chalked her cue stick and looked at him. "That's what you wanted, wasn't it? For Stretch and Junior and Bulldog to like it here? You seduced them, didn't you? Now was that fair?"

"Seemed like a good idea. You're mad about that, are you?"

"Oh, yeah."

"Too bad. They're enjoying themselves and I like having them around."

"Sure. Nightly poker and checker games, fantastic dinners, a hot tub, sailing—it's a regular playground around here. At this rate, they'll never get back to their careers. That was underhanded, Stepanov."

"That's their choice. So how is your work going?"

She angled a shot, bounced the ball off the cushioned rim to nudge another ball into the pocket. "Haven't been. Seems I'm out of focus. That hasn't happened to me before."

Danya sat to watch and placed his boots up on the table nearby. He considered her bottom as she took a shot. "Wearing anything under that?"

Sidney stopped to look at him. "Not a thing."

Danya decided to go straight for the problem between them. "If you think that getup is going to make me forget that you walked off and left me, didn't call, or send me flowers, you're dead wrong. You came at me too fast last time, and I wasn't prepared for that, but now I am."

"I wasn't exactly expecting that first time, either. I was feeling—unusual. And you bought a house, and everyone knew that you had someone in mind to live in it with you."

"You came here, in that getup to have it out, didn't you? I explained that to you before: it was a good price and a good time. I'm a house sort of guy, whether anyone lives in it with me, or not. Maybe I did have big ideas about you. Maybe they're gone now."

"You're bristling, Stepanov. You're usually Mr. Cool and Easy."

"You've changed things, brought out the worst in me." Danya thought of how Sidney had been, coming at him full speed on the dance floor; he shouldn't have taken her that night, but he did and now the relationship-road was bumpy and filled with potential hazards. In fact, Sidney was a real hazard—unpredictable and very fast, once she'd made up her mind.

He stood and moved around the tavern, closing it for the night, leaving only the light above the pool table.

She watched him chose a cue stick from the rack and chalk it. "It seems like a hundred years ago."

"Maybe to you. You've been on the move. Running scared, I'd say."

In the shadows, Sidney's face caught the red light blinking from the window's neon sign. "My family has changed. We've never been together in a house before. It's usually a hotel, or a suite or camping."

"Maybe you're the one who's changed. Eight ball?" Danya racked the balls, the eight ball in the center of the triangle. "Take the break," he said, indicating the cue ball which would be shot into the triangle of solid and striped balls. "Solids or stripes?"

Sidney turned to him and placed her cue stick aside. "You," she said simply. "I want you. A rematch where you get that romance you need."

Because Danya was off balance, feeling delicate after being poleaxed by Sidney once again, he needed to think through his reaction to her "rematch." Danya lined up the cue ball and shot forcefully into the triangle. The balls spread across the green baize surface of the table. He circled the table, angled for a shot and pocketed two balls. "Just like that. You want me. Drop into Amoteh, visit with your family, and then have me. Now that is really interesting. I'll tell you what I want—you to stick around long enough to go to my aunt and uncle's wedding anniversary at the end of the week. They like you, the whole family does. Think of it as a—"

He looked directly at her before taking another shot and took a leap that could frighten her. "As a date. Just a family get-together, food, fun and folk dancing. It would mean a lot to my father to see you there."

"But would it mean a lot to you?" Sidney asked hesitantly and moved to place her hands on his chest, looking up at him, her eyes filling with him.

Cautious of his reaction to her closeness, that unique woman-scent arousing him, Danya moved away from her to pocket more balls, shooting both solids and stripes because he was afraid he'd move too fast with her…and because he was frustrated, two emotions that he rarely had known before Sidney. He pocketed the eight ball last and then turned to her. "I'm not asking for a thing. Everything is your decision. But here's how I see it: We moved too fast, sex was good, but the foundation was poor. For my part, I said once that I'd take what I could get, and I still mean that."

Danya tossed his cue stick to the pool table on his way to Sidney, and tugged her into his arms.

She met his hunger with her own, her lips feasting on his, parted for him, slanted to fit, her arms locked around his neck. Danya cupped the back of her head with one hand, holding her tight against him with his other arm, his hand open and digging in possessively. It had been too long…and Sidney was everything, soft and fragrant and hungry, making those sweet little noises at the back of her throat. When his arms went around her waist, lifting her off the floor, Sidney held him tight.

Then she pushed him slightly away, and her hands framed his face. "This isn't right," she whispered unevenly.

Danya caressed her bottom, drawing her tight against his need. "It feels right."

"When we first met, you said you needed romance. Foreplay, after play, all that stuff. And you like lovemaking, not just hurried sex. You're very thorough in everything you do. I'm not. I'm more of an—an observer, not moving into life, rather hurrying along the perimeter, taking what I can get."

Her earnest expression caught him and he sensed that Sidney was on the brink of some new plan—and that made him uneasy. Was she getting ready to leave already? "So?"

"So, I'd like to try getting into the stream of things, explore opportunities, yada, yada. In spite of you nabbing my family and changing them, you deserve more than a hit and run affair—that's what I'm geared for, or was. This time, I'd like a little more time to—smell those roses. I'm sure not on the rebound from Ben now, and I'd like a rematch, Stepanov. If my family can live with you, I guess I can, too—just to see what happens. Is it a deal?"

"You living with me? I can handle that," he agreed slowly as he lowered her to the floor. Sidney seemed uneasy and he pressed— "And? What else?"

She lay close to him, her head resting on his chest, as if she'd come home from a very long journey. Danya closed his arms around her, nuzzled her hair, and got a little dizzy with pleasure. "Whatever is bothering you, sweetheart, we'll work through it."

"What if I—what if I can't make it here? What if I don't fit in?"

"Then I'll love you."

"No promises, Danya. All I can do is to try. But I—I guess I just might love you, too."

His throat tightened with emotion, but he managed a rough, "Good enough."

"I'd sure like to make love now, Danya," she whispered unevenly.

"Oh, you would, would you?" he asked as he picked Sidney up in his arms and started up the stairs leading to the area above the tavern.

"Just to—you know to cement the deal, me living with you. You love this, don't you? Playing macho man when I'm perfectly able to—"

In the barren spacious area above the bar, Danya placed her on her feet, letting her choose the moment to come to him. Sidney walked slowly around the room, passing the huge Stepanov bed sometimes used for guests. Then her silhouette crossed in front of the massive windows and her booted feet walked across the squares of moonlight painted on the bare wooden boards. She stopped and braced one boot on a chair, unlacing it and then doing the same with the other, dropping them to the floor in turn. Moving gracefully, she removed her clothing and slowly crossed the distance of the night's shadows to Danya. "I missed you so much—"

Her hands slid to his shirt, unbuttoning it slowly, removing it to skim his shoulders, his chest. Then she tugged at his belt, and when she failed to release it, bent to look closely at the buckle. "What's with this thing?"

Danya was having difficulty breathing and in one quick motion, freed the buckle. "You were saying?"

"Oh, my," she whispered as she unzipped his jeans, sliding her hands over his hips and then finding him—

Danya looked up at the ceiling and promised himself that this time he would move slowly, surely—

But Sidney was already moving upon him.

So much for patience, Danya mocked himself as he carried her to the bed.

So much for patience and gentleness, he decided as Sidney caught him, her body welcoming his instantly.

So much for patience, Danya thought again, as he lost himself in her….

Sidney came instantly, furiously into her storm, tightening upon him. Danya fought desperately back from the brink of release, watched her go into herself, that wide helpless stare as her body contracted.

"We're going to have to work on this, dear heart," he managed rawly before he began caressing her breasts, nibbling the tender peaks and keeping himself reined in until she started moving restlessly above him.

"I just want you so much, all of you. It seems a shame to waste more time—"

"Does it?" he asked, turning her beneath him. "Have I told you how much I love the shape of your ears?" he asked as he bent to nuzzle and nibble.

"No, but yours are nice. Tan. Big. I suppose they'll get hair in them as you age." Her hands skimmed his shoulders. "I imagine you'll get hair on your shoulders, too. Bulldog has to have the hair in his ears and nose trimmed, and he's got a lot of hair on his shoulders. Men do that, you know. Women sag and men grow hair in the wrong places."

Danya smiled against her throat and slid his hands beneath her bottom, rocking her gently against him. He nuzzled her breasts. "I love it when you talk dirty."

"Um. You're still busy with the project, aren't you?"

"Like you said, I'm a thorough sort of guy."

"I think that while we're—on our deal thingie—that I'm going to touch you more. Ben never liked—"

Danya stopped moving and braced his weight on his elbows above her. "Big mistake, my darling," he reminded her very quietly.

"Oops."

"Yes, oops."

"Don't you dare start that bristling, noise out of joint, man-thing—you know I love you—I think—and we're doing the handshake on a deal thing now, aren't we? I'm sorry, Danya, that I hurt you. Really I am," she whispered fiercely as she gripped his face and brought him down to her lips, pasting a flurry of kisses over his face. "I'm going to romance the hell out of you, seduce you slowly, thoroughly, and—"

Danya was floating happily, both from her promises, and from her body. "Tell me that part again—that you love me and I'll consider it."

Sidney grinned and lifted slightly to nip his shoulder. She lay back down and her grin widened as she wiggled beneath him. "Make me."

Ten

At dawn, Bulldog was standing on Danya's deck, his coffee mug in hand as he watched Sidney and Danya walk up from the shoreline.

Danya's arm was tight around Sidney, his expression grim beneath the stubble covering his jaw. Sidney knew what her father was seeing: She was wearing Danya's cotton shirt over her sports bra; she looked rumpled and soft and tucked close against the man she'd spent the night with, who'd had her three times, and who had just shown her that there was a very small, but intimate button within a woman's body that when touched at just the right moment could—

Sidney met her father's appraising look and blushed, but she held her head high. When they stopped at the bottom of the wooden steps leading up to the deck, she said, "We're going for a rematch. Danya needs romance and I'm going to give it to him. He's delicate that way, and don't you dare hurt him, Bulldog. And you can call off Stretch and Junior."

At her side, Danya frowned down at her. "I don't need your

protection, dear heart," he grumbled in that bristling-male cute-guy thing she loved so much.

"It's my family. I'll handle this."

"Just maybe we could handle it together?" he asked between his teeth.

"So that's how it is, huh?" her father asked gruffly. "You think you can handle this kind of life—because it wouldn't be fair to him, if you couldn't. You can't just pick up and leave him high and dry. This guy is sensitive."

Danya's arm drew Sidney closer, protectively against him as they moved up the steps to the deck. "There's a marriage offer on the table and I'll take what I can get."

"That's what her mother said to me years ago. Sid is a lot like my wife was—once she's made up her mind, she usually goes for it, and fast, too." Over Sidney's head, Bulldog's eyes locked with Danya's. "The problem is, my girls have a lot of me in them, too. And that makes life hard for the one waiting at home."

Unsteady with her emotions and still feeling sated and soft and feminine, Sidney suddenly felt overwhelmed and terrified. "No one said anything about getting married, Bulldog...Danya. We're just in a rematch here, working through things. I might not fit into—"

Danya sighed heavily and kissed the top of Sidney's head. "She's scared, Roy. We're going to take some time getting used to what we've got."

Bulldog nodded slowly. "Sounds like a plan."

"I am not scared," Sidney stated in her defense, a little angry that the men seemed to be settling her life between them. "And Danya always has a plan. He's very thorough— and that takes a lot of time."

Danya's big hand caressed her waist and onto her hip, reminding her just how effective he could be in his slow and thorough mode. Sensitized by a night of lovemaking, Sidney's body did that instant warming, alert and waiting hungrily tense quiver.

Then it was true, she decided: *Men did have power over women. She could have become Danya's love slave.* She eyed him cautiously and moved away, only to be drawn back again, patiently, firmly.

"So how is this going to work, son?" Bulldog asked as he poured a cup of coffee from the thermal pot and handed it to Danya. "I just want to know that my little girl—"

"I'm thirty years old, Roy. I can handle myself," Sidney stated firmly.

"See? She's all defensive now, or she wouldn't have called me 'Roy,'" Bulldog said. "A fighter, just like her mother. The problem is, I didn't raise Sid to fit in a regular mold and I don't want her crying all over the place like she has been doing. It's goddamn unnerving when women cry. I can't take much of that."

Danya sipped his coffee, let out a pleasured, "Ah." He sprawled in a wooden deck chair and lifted his feet to rest upon the railing. "I thought we'd all live here together. That way you'd feel more comfortable with our arrangement, Roy. Not that you have to, but if you wanted, you could call this your home. You like fishing with Uncle Fadey and my dad, and you seem to like it here. You may as well stay. It's a nice place to retire."

Sidney looked at her father who had never contemplated staying anywhere very long. She didn't expect his answer: "Maybe grow things, help keep up the rose garden, that sort of thing?" Bulldog asked with interest.

"It's a big house and a big bunch of land, Roy. I'd appreciate your help."

Sidney stared at the two men who were making plans without her. She hadn't even gotten into her new relationship/rematch with Danya and he and her father were agreeing on living together— "Wait a minute…*wait a minute*—what about me? Where do I fit in?"

Danya smiled at her in a way that she didn't trust. "Anywhere you like, my darling. Just anywhere you like. Everything is up to you."

"Well—" She could feel herself huffing, adrift in this whole new bright, overwhelming and terrifying morning. "I'm not the usual housewifey kind of woman, you know. What if things go wrong? What if you and I don't work out? I mean I love you, but I can't put Bulldog into a position where if things don't work out, he's uncomfortable staying here. He's not that young and has to live someplace he's comfortable in—roses, my gosh, Bulldog, when did you ever think about growing roses?"

Bulldog grumbled and looked fiercely defensive. "Lots of men grow flowers."

"Not you."

"Hell, I can if I want to."

Danya reached to pat Sidney's bottom. "Why don't you go see about your sisters, sweetheart? I'd like to talk to your father alone."

She looked at him in disbelief. "Let me get this straight— you're sending me to my room?"

"It's a man-thing," Danya said easily. "Roy and I have some fine-tuning to do on our new living arrangement."

Sidney understood immediately and fought the blush rising up her cheeks. *Living arrangement—as in who sleeps where.* Thirty years old or not, she just couldn't tell her father that she needed to spend every night in Danya's arms; she'd wasted enough time rummaging through life to find him and she wasn't sleeping away from him. "Oh. Oh, well. I just will then…go inside."

Stretch and Junior were already playing pool, dressed in familiar men's cotton shirts that had an odd pink tinge. "What are you doing, wearing Danya's shirts?" Sidney demanded.

"He said it was okay. Stretch tried to do the laundry—another one of those dumb bets we lost—and put some red stuff in with Danya's shirts. They're ours now. But he didn't seem to mind his pink undershorts—seems to be a go-with-the-flow sort of guy. You look like you've been rolled over and had but good," Junior noted with interest. "I've never seen you looking all soft and cuddly. Good gosh, the next thing you know you'll be chucking out babies. Those Stepanov men are proven baby makers, Sid. You'd better watch your step and you'd better get something to eat before you fall on your face. Bulldog has been cooking for a couple hours. He loves that snazzy new kitchen."

"That's good, because he's going to live here. Everyone's invited," Sidney stated darkly as she walked into the kitchen. "Now, I'm never going to get any time alone with Danya. How am I ever going to give him the romance he needs under my family's noses?" she muttered.

From the breakfast Bulldog had laid out, Sidney spooned blueberries onto a pancake; she drank orange juice and studied the recipes stuck to the refrigerator with magnets—Bulldog had written notes on the paper and had made a grocery list. A pasta maker sat next to a recipe book on Italian cooking. Her sisters came into the kitchen and Stretch leaned against the door frame while Junior dived into the food Sidney had just prepared. "How does this work?" Sidney asked her sisters. "Everyone living here? Together?"

"Great. Both Bulldog and Danya cook and do laundry—except for when we lost that poker bet. The Stepanovs are card sharks, too. Apparently all there is to do on their Montana ranch in the winter time is to play cards and pool…. Bulldog is great at laundry. Do you know he can fold diapers a mile a minute and stack them perfectly? And you should see him diaper babies. He's a real whiz and said he used to enjoy all that stuff with us. Who would know?"

Sidney drank the remainder of her orange juice. "I'm moving in. I'm in a tight rematch situation and I'm going to sleep with Danya. How's that going to work, me trying to romance him, with my whole family living here?"

Junior shrugged. "Beats me. I never tried to romance anyone."

"Not a clue," Stretch said.

Clearly Sidney's sisters had never worried about long, slow, thorough lovemaking, which could end by hearing ones own high, keening sound of pleasure.

"Let's take this stuff out onto the porch and watch the sun come up. We've got just enough time before we have to go," Junior said around her mouthful of pancake.

"Go where?" Sidney asked hopefully. Perhaps her sisters had to get back to their careers, and then just maybe Bulldog would get restless and want to visit them, thus leaving Sidney to experiment in seducing Danya.

"Climbing that cliff up to Strawberry Hill. Boys against the girls. And if any packages come today, don't open them. We ordered some girly clothes, some really slutty looking stuff…push-up bras, the whole works. That ought to knock them on their butts, because they think women should be sweet." Stretch's evil grin said that Sergei and Kiril weren't going to like the "girly clothes."

Alone in the kitchen, Sidney stabbed her pancake, cut it into pieces and jammed some into her mouth. She was chewing on her next move when Danya came into the kitchen and bent to kiss her. He had a pleased smile she didn't trust. "You're looking all chipper, Stepanov," she noted cautiously.

"Got to get to work. New job. Nice profit." He poured a glass of orange juice. "What are you going to do today?"

"The big question is what's happening here, honey-bun-lover. We're all going to live here—together, my family and you and me? How's this going to work?"

"People do it all the time. They're worried about you. This gives everyone a chance to adjust."

"Mmm."

"Problem?"

"Yes, a big one. How am I going to tell you I love you, and how are we—you know—going to, um, make love?"

"Up to you, I guess. Your call." Finished with his orange juice and pancake, Danya reached for her and lifted her up, carrying her into the laundry room and closing the door as he sat her on the washer, which was agitating, matching the hum that had started low in her body. Danya's big hands were busy caressing her breasts slowly, effectively, running those thumbs across her nipples. "Take it easy today, okay, sweetheart? You look tired and maybe a little dazed."

Sidney locked her legs around his hips and her arms around his shoulders. "You should know why."

"Can't you handle it?"

He grinned and Sidney's heart flip-flopped wildly. "You? Anytime."

"Keep that thought," he whispered after he'd given her a long, devastating kiss. "See you tonight."

When he had gone to shower and dress for work, Sidney sat on that washer until Bulldog came into the laundry room. He took the clothes from the dryer and folded them on a work table. "Old diapers make the best dust cloths, you know," he said quietly.

"Uh-huh... What did you and Danya talk about outside, Bulldog?" Sidney asked.

"Stuff men talk about."

Sidney noted the tears in her father's eyes and the way he sniffed roughly. "Sure. What am I going to do here, Dad? I mean, I have to do something, don't I?"

"Oh, something will come along."

"You talked about Mom just now. It's not like you to say much. Is something bothering you?"

"I miss her now and then...you, more than the other girls, are like her. I was thinking as I saw you and Danya this morning, how it happened the same way with your mother and me. Fast. I was so eager to get her that maybe I skipped a few of the important things that Danya wants for you."

"It's a whole big package here, Bulldog. In a family like the Stepanovs, women are supposed to—well, they do women-things. And I'm scared," Sidney admitted slowly.

"And that's my fault. You girls should have had a mother, a woman in your life, easing out the rough spots. If you don't think you can manage with us here, then we'll leave. But Sid, he's a good man, trying hard to do right by you."

Sidney hugged her father, who remained stiff in her arms for just that moment before he returned the hug. She realized how different the Blakelys were from the Stepanovs who demonstrated affection easily. "What if I let him down, Dad? What if I'm not what he needs? What if someday, some good job comes along, maybe a real career maker, and I want to take it?"

Bulldog's arms tightened around her. "I guess that's between you and him."

Sidney walked slowly into Danya's bedroom and closed the door.

The spacious room held the scent of his shower and Sidney wandered to her little vanity, sitting upon it. She was alone in the room she would share with Danya tonight and every other night they were together.

The big bed reflected in the mirror behind her was neatly made, a large patchwork quilt covering it, a bed where she would spend her nights with Danya.

Outside, Bulldog was working in the yard and birds were chirping. Stretch and Junior were off climbing with Sergei and Kiril on Strawberry Hill's cliff. Everything seemed so normal—and yet so foreign. Sidney studied her reflection, a woman who had spent the night loving a man, giving herself to him, a woman who looked terrified and in unfamiliar surroundings.

Could she make Danya happy?

Could she give him what he needed?

Could she share her life as well as her body with him?

Who was she?

Sidney hurried out to the living room where she'd stacked her travel bag and camera gear; she carried them back to the spacious bedroom, stepped inside, and closed the door. This would be her first-ever, very private room with Danya. She placed the bags on the bed and headed for the shower that carried his scent. The soap she used on her body was still wet from Danya's and she rubbed it all over, remembering his slow, erotic caresses of the previous night. Drying slowly, Sidney walked into the bedroom, dressed in Danya's T-shirt and shorts, then sat at the little vanity. She ran her hands over the smooth walnut surface and thought about Danya lying in bed behind her, watching her brush her hair as he had said....

He'd given her a gift he'd made with his own hands, a real statement, and that troubled Sidney. She had no skills in the sweetheart business. On impulse, she hurried to her camera bag, found the Stepanov family's glossy prints and hurried into the kitchen, rummaging until she found thumb tacks. Sidney hurried back to the bedroom and tacked the pictures all over the wall above the bed.

Then she lay down at the opposite end of the bed, wrapped the quilt around her and studied the large glossy pictures. It was the best of herself that she could give Danya. "Good composition. Good subjects."

With a sigh of satisfaction that she had redecorated his room, Sidney slid into sleep.

Danya held his breath as he walked into his home that evening.

Sidney had brought him lunch, a somewhat flattened and battered peanut butter and jam sandwich, and he'd quietly hid the hearty turkey and cheese sub sandwich that Jessica had made for him. Sidney had been quiet and he realized suddenly that she was now shy of him; she'd sat beside him near the new dormer windows on the roof, and surveyed the ocean, the beach, the children playing on it, the tourists milling on the pier, and then she'd put her arm around him as they sat side by side.

Danya had held very still, absorbing this new intimate gesture. She had smiled shyly at him. "Good sandwich. Thanks," he'd said.

"Alexi is eating a great big one."

"This is better." Her hand had slid up to his hair, toying with it, and then she'd placed her head lightly on his shoulder. Danya had understood immediately that she was experimenting. A woman raised in a family that rarely showed affection by touching, she'd come to him and she was nervous of this new beginning. Danya had taken her hand and Sidney took it to her lap, studying the broad dark width against her own. "Nice. Different."

She'd looked at his bare chest and had started to breathe quickly, her eyes going almost black. "Sweaty. Smooth. You'd be very slick if—"

Danya had jackknifed to his feet, because if he didn't, they'd be making love right on the roof. "Well, better get back to work. Let me help you off the roof."

"Hey, guy. I'm not helpless." But Sidney had blushed and hurried away from him.

All afternoon, he'd held that image of Sidney's large dark eyes on his chest, the way her tongue came out to slide over her bottom lip as if she'd like to taste him. At quitting time, Danya had hurried home, anxious to see her.

In the house, Stretch and Junior were modeling their girly-clothes, tight and low cut, their faces overly painted, and getting ready to go out on the date that was intended to mortify his cousins. Sidney's sisters didn't know Sergei and Kiril very well. When the cousins arrived soon after, Bulldog served iced tea and talked comfortably with the men.

Sergei grinned at Danya and winked.

"My, how lovely you look," Kiril said to the sisters.

"You lost the climbing race, too, huh?" Sidney asked with a grin.

Stretch turned on her like a tiger. "You think you could do any better, short stuff?"

"I've always been faster than you guys in something like that. Less weight to haul, more agile, yada, yada."

After the couples left, Danya took his shower and Bulldog served dinner, a shrimp and linguine dish from his new spiffy Italian recipe book. Sidney pulled out Danya's chair for him to sit and then sat beside him. She took his hand and held it on the table. "How do people eat like this?" she asked curiously.

"Well, that takes practice," Bulldog answered, diving into his own food.

He seemed to enjoy listening to the projects Danya and Alexi had contracted, and was just serving dessert when the door burst open and Stretch and Junior stomped in, carrying their high heels. "We're leaving in the morning," Junior said. "Paid all the damn debts we owe to your cousins, Danya. What's to eat? Mmm. Pasta."

"I thought you'd stay out late," Sidney stated tightly as the sisters sat to eat hungrily. "I thought you'd be cooking and cleaning at the cabin."

"Oh, we cooked," Stretch said. "These guys are from Montana and they didn't like burned steaks and who knew you had to wash potatoes before you baked them?"

"It was sheer hell," Junior said, "Got to haul out of here in the early morning. Back to work."

"You could leave tonight," Sidney suggested in that tight, furious tone.

"Stay as long as you like," Danya invited, and she turned to scowl at him.

"Well, hell, girls, I thought you liked it here," Bulldog said. "But if that's how it goes, what about a game of pool after dinner. You, Danya? You, Sid?"

After the first game ended, Sidney faked a yawn and slid a sultry look at Danya that said she wanted him and she couldn't wait any longer. "I'm hitting the sack."

The Blakelys barely noticed Sidney and Danya walking to their bedroom. Inside, Danya locked the door. Sidney was showing all the signs of a nervous bride, keeping her distance from him. She may have wanted him earlier on a sensual plane, but now she was wary of him in this new intimate, seemingly semipermanent relationship.

It would be their first night in his home, in his bed, and that held connotations that evidently still frightened Sidney. He'd give her all the time she needed to adjust to this intimacy. He surveyed the large glossy family pictures tacked over his bed.

"Thanks for decorating. I didn't know what to do with the walls."

"You're welcome. I stuck up a few in your office, too, and in the living room. You may have noticed. This afternoon, I took some of Bulldog's roses, really nice still shots, zoomed right in there. Tomorrow morning, I might even catch a drop of dew. Sometimes dew on spider webs can sparkle like jewels.... Danya?"

"Hmm?"

"Um—I think I'll take a shower."

"Okay."

"Don't go back and play pool or anything, will you?"

"I was thinking about it," he said, just to see how she reacted. Sidney always reacted perfectly.

She walked slowly to him and Danya held his breath while she lifted her arms and placed them around his shoulders. "Hi," she whispered and stood on tiptoe to whisper in his ear. "Honey," she added softly.

Danya's hands tightened on her waist. It was the first endearment she'd given him. His heart did that racing thing because he knew it was the first "Honey" she'd given to anyone.

She brushed her lips across his on her way to his other ear. "Hi—dear."

Then she rested her head upon his shoulder, snuggling to him as she smoothed his back with her open hands. Adrift in sweet sensations, Danya held her against him. "Hi, yourself."

Sidney leaned back to look up at him, and smooth his hair back from his face. "You're such a sweet guy. Really. I mean it."

She stood on tiptoe again and lightly kissed his lips, his jaw, his throat. Danya realized that she was experimenting in her romantic technique, but he was having an immediate and urgent problem, his body hardening. He groaned slightly, wondering how long he could restrain himself from making love to her.

Sidney began to unbutton his shirt and with each button leaned to place a kiss on his chest, his stomach, and she was taking too long— Danya smiled tightly as she turned to look up at him with that drowsy shy and impish look. "This is going to take a very long time, honey. Relax. You're so tense and hot and fierce already. I'll be back in just a minute—"

She left him rigid and shaking and dazed as she walked to the dresser. She slid away her T-shirt and sports bra and shimmied out of her jeans and undershorts. Danya couldn't move, pinned to the sight of Sidney's pale curved body, moving gracefully as she slid into a short black negligee, supported by two tiny straps. She stepped delicately into a ruffled scrap of cloth and turned to him. "What do you think? Does this look romantic? I found it in a shop on my way to bring you lunch."

Danya had that fierce hot look she loved, but Sidney had promised to take her time romancing him. She walked to the vanity he'd made for her, sat down and picked up a brush. In the mirror, Danya stood rigidly behind her. "How much time is this going to take?"

"Why, honey, I really don't know. I'm new at this, you know."

"Pick up the pace, my darling," he ordered huskily.

"Now there's a time for everything. Romance can't be rushed—"

"You're killing me, Sid." Danya sat on the bed, kicked off his shoes, slid off his socks and stood to unzip his jeans, sliding out of them and his shorts. He threw back the quilt and sheet, turned and studied her.

Sidney continued to slowly brush her hair. "This anticipation stuff really works, huh? Building the moment and all that? A slow seduction, rather than just going for it?"

With a rough sigh, Danya turned off the light, lay down on the bed and covered his hips and legs with a sheet. He placed his hands behind his head and watched her. Sidney took her time applying moisturizer to her hands and then to her body, making certain that Danya had full view of her legs. "Come to bed, my darling," he ordered roughly.

"In a minute—"

"Now."

Thoroughly enjoying tantalizing Danya—a patient man who always took his time, but now couldn't wait—Sidney smiled in the night's shadows. "But I thought you might want to go play pool with my family. Have you changed your mind?"

Danya sprang out of bed, walked to the vanity and scooped her up in his arms. He tossed Sidney lightly upon the bed and she smiled her best sultry one up at him. Certain that he was going to have her in his arms, Danya smiled back and bent to slide into bed with her.

Sidney scooted out, and Danya was faster than she expected, reaching for her. He was laughing now, a good sound, and Sidney knew that he'd make a perfect playmate—therefore, she just had to dive upon him. Danya caught her and held her tight as he lay on his side, smiling at her.

"I'd appreciate it if you'd—you know, make certain I didn't scream or anything," Sidney whispered. "You don't want Bulldog and my sisters worried about me, do you?"

"This room is soundproof. I turned up the radio in here today, stood in the hallway and listened—not a sound. And I love those noises you make—can't get enough of them." Danya was busy stroking away the filmy negligee, his hand smoothing her hip, her thigh. "Call me 'honey,' and see what you get."

Sidney smiled back at him. "Honey?"

His expression stilled as he said quietly, "I love you, Sidney. I loved you from the first time I saw you."

His quiet declaration caught her, wrapping around her heart. "I love you, too."

"Mmm." Danya sighed, and still holding her against him, lay back against the pillows, covering them with a sheet.

Sidney listened to the slow beating of his heart and smoothed his chest. "I love you, Danya," she whispered again, more firmly this time, adjusting to the words on her lips, because she was going to give him plenty of them.

They lay there in the night, close and tender, and then

Danya began to make love to her with long sweet kisses that heated and warmed.

He was making this first time in his home, very special, she realized as his lips moved to one ear and then the other, and then slowly down to her throat. Those beautiful big wide hands moved gently over her, easing her closer, soothing her as she began to tremble and hold him tight. She held her breath as Danya nuzzled her stomach and lower.

When Sidney could stand no more, her fingers digging into his shoulders, her head tossing upon the pillow, her hips lifting restlessly, eagerly, Danya worked his way back up to her breasts again. He treated gently, thoroughly, tugging at her with lips and teeth and flicking his tongue over the sensitized peaks.

Sidney smoothed that rock-hard stomach and found the full hot silky length of him. Burning with the fever now consuming them both, she urged Danya to complete her. She moved quickly through her storm, the fever pounding, threshing them, skin against damp skin, softness and muscle, plunging desperately against him, aware of his lips, his mouth slanted perfectly to hers as were their bodies....

Textures, smooth and hard, stroked her body, Danya's hands cupping her bottom, lifting her higher to meet him, withdrawing, joining—

She seemed to ride those pleasured peaks forever, distantly aware of his uneven breath, of his straining to hold her. Then everything stopped, whirled around them, and suddenly, he came down to her arms, damp and heavy, and he belonged to her.

Sidney stroked Danya's muscled back, soothed his trembling body, eased his damp hair from his face, listened to his uneven breathing against her throat, and gave herself to the peace of coming home. "Mmm," she whispered against his cheek, "I'm not the only one who can't keep quiet. There was this muffled little shout at the end."

"I was saving it just for you," he murmured in a drowsy tone that said she'd taken everything, met him on an equal plane, demanded everything back. It was quite the fulfilling feeling, on top of being quite pleasured herself, to know that she'd given him everything, that she'd taken everything.

Sidney forced her hand to flop to the side, and Danya chuckled deeply, easing away slightly, until her head lay on his chest, her limbs tangled with his. Danya caressed her head, his fingers working magic, until she slid into sleep.

During the night, Sidney heard the shower running and rose to enter the bedroom's spacious bathroom. Danya's tall fit body moved beyond the glass closure. She leaned against the vanity, studying him, thinking how wonderful he was, this lover of hers, when the glass door opened and Danya's hand circled her wrist— "In."

In the tiny space, he seemed even larger and somehow foreign and fierce as the shower spray hit his head, plastering his hair close. Danya carefully, intently, soaped and rinsed her body with minute care. Embarrassed that he should be so attentive, almost as if he were tending a child, Sidney stepped back and closed her arms over her breasts. "That's enough."

"Is it?" Danya asked too quietly. "You're still shy of me, aren't you? After all this?"

"This is new. Different. It's very intimate. I—I'm a private person."

"We have been that…intimate…. Okay." Danya stepped out of the shower enclosure, leaving her alone in the spray and the steam.

Finished with her shower, Sidney noted the soft woman in the mirror and sighed. Danya had been very thorough, and her face was still flushed from lovemaking and exhaustion, but there were shadows around her eyes and her body felt relaxed. She wrapped in a large thick towel and when he wasn't in the bedroom, wandered onto the bedroom's tiny private deck to find him sitting in a wooden recliner.

Sidney understood immediately that he'd come here to brood while she was gone and she ached to soothe that loneliness now. She eased onto his lap and Danya drew her close, kissing her forehead. She lay very still, absorbing this new phase, the quiet, good one where no words were needed.

"This is good. I hope I don't turn into a clinging Fluffy-type woman."

"Cling all you want. Look," Danya said, indicating the direction with a nod of his head. There, on a bench in the moonlight, overlooking the ocean, were three familiar shapes. Bulldog sat with an arm around each daughter.

"I'll miss them."

"This is their home now, too, you know. I just ask that they don't try to renovate until they consult me. I've got a suspicion that when your sisters decide they are going to change something—they do."

Danya framed Sidney's chin with his hand and turned her to look at him. "I meant what I said about taking whatever I could get. That doesn't mean you'll be tied down here, if you need to travel."

"I'm happy here, now with you, honey," she whispered shyly.

"Uh-huh. But if the time comes, you'll let me know, won't you? And by the way, I'm not repeating that offer of marriage."

She toyed with the fascinating center of his chin, kissing it. "Some offer. You asked my father, and then me. 'Well, will you?' you said."

"I think you can be more romantic—if you feel like it. But only when you feel it is right for you."

"Well, will you?" Sidney asked slowly, carefully. "Marry me?"

Epilogue

After Danya and Sidney's September beach wedding, the photographer kissed the groom, stood on tiptoe to whisper she loved him, and hurried toward her camera equipment.

In a flurry of his mother's traditional lace dress and a lacy veil, Sidney came running back to Danya. On her way, she stopped to kiss Bulldog, Viktor and Fadey. She stood on tiptoe to whisper something into Viktor's ear and tears came to his eyes before he turned to speak Fadey and Bulldog. They looked soft and humbled and Bulldog brushed away a tear. "I wonder what she said," Alexi murmured.

"She wants boys—three. Their namesakes, and if it's girls, well, she'll get inventive."

Alexi chuckled. "She's a fast mover. Get prepared, brother."

"Oh, I am."

Rosy with excitement, Sidney hurried on to Danya who was standing by his brother. "Alexi, give your brother his bouquet. I've just got to get this shot."

Alexi grinned and handed the huge bouquet of roses to Danya. "Your wedding bouquet, Danya?" he asked in a way that said he wasn't going to stop teasing Danya for a long time.

Danya only smiled; nothing mattered except the love—and romance—Sidney seemed set upon giving him.

"You looked great carrying it. Oh, wait a minute—" Sidney ordered.

She eased his arms away from his body and stepped in close to smooth his newly embroidered festival shirt that now matched all the other Stepanov males.

His bride was truly romantic, handing him the rose bouquet she'd given him to carry as he walked toward her and their marriage.

Sidney studied him critically, straightened the wide collar, and smiled softly up at him. He'd remember that glowing smile forever, Danya thought, the way her eyes cherished him. With his arms wide-open, he bent to take a long, thorough kiss that would hold him over until they were alone, and Sidney held very still.

Then as if remembering her work, she leaned back, smoothed his hair in a touch that reflected a wife's pride and possession. She urged his arms down, smoothed the billowing full sleeves of his festival shirt, and arranged his hands and the bouquet for the shot she wanted.

Sidney considered his look, smoothed his face with the hand that wore her new wedding ring, and took a rose bud from the bouquet. She broke the stem and placed it over his ear. She kissed him again, her eyes filling with him and the lifetime of happiness they would have together.

"Now hold that thought," she whispered softly, and Danya knew she wasn't talking about the pose....

* * * * *

THE CRENSHAWS OF TEXAS
**Brothers bound by blood
and the land they call home!**

DOUBLE IDENTITY
(Silhouette Desire #1646,
available April 2005)
by Annette Broadrick

Undercover agent Jude Crenshaw
had only gotten involved with
Carina Patterson for the sake of
cracking a smuggling case against
her brothers. But close quarters soon
led to a shared attraction, and Jude
could only hope his double identity
wouldn't break both their hearts.

*Available at your
favorite retail outlet.*

DYNASTIES : THE ASHTONS

**A family built on lies…
brought together by dark,
passionate secrets.**

JUST A TASTE

(Silhouette Desire #1645,
available April 2005)

by Bronwyn Jameson

When Jillian Ashton's arrogant
husband died, it wasn't long before
she found a man who treated her
right—*really* right. Problem was,
Seth—a tall, dark and handsome
hunk—was her late husband's
brother. She'd planned on just
a taste of his tender touch, but
was left wanting more….

*Available at your
favorite retail outlet.*

presents

BEYOND BUSINESS

(SD #1649, April 2005)

by Rochelle Alers

The sizzling conclusion of

THE BLACKSTONES OF VIRGINIA

Seduction is on the agenda for patriarch
Sheldon Blackstone when he learns his new secretary
is sexy *and* expecting! A widower who never thought
he'd have a second chance at love, Sheldon must
convince the commitment-wary career woman to
trust her heart and begin a new family with him on
his sprawling, glamorous plantation.

Available at your favorite retail outlet.

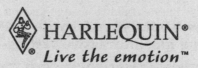

COMING NEXT MONTH

#1645 JUST A TASTE—Bronwyn Jameson
Dynasties: The Ashtons
When Jillian Ashton's arrogant husband died, it wasn't long before she found a man who treated her right—*really* right. Problem was, Seth—a tall, dark and handsome hunk—was her late husband's brother. She'd planned on just a taste of his tender touch, but was left wanting more....

#1646 DOUBLE IDENTITY—Annette Broadrick
The Crenshaws of Texas
Undercover agent Jude Crenshaw only meant to attract Carina Patterson for the sake of cracking a case against her brothers. But when close quarters turned his business into their pleasure, Jude could only hope his double identity wouldn't turn their new union into two broken hearts.

#1647 RULES OF ATTRACTION—Susan Crosby
Behind Closed Doors
P.I. Quinn Gerard was following a suspected accomplice—or so he thought. When the sexy bombshell turned out to be her twin sister, Claire, Quinn no longer had to watch her every move. But he couldn't seem to take his eyes off her! Could Quinn convince Claire to bend the rules and give in to their mutual attraction?

#1648 WHEN THE EARTH MOVES—Roxanne St. Claire
After Jo Ellen Tremaine's best friend died during an earthquake, she was determined to adopt her friend's baby girl. But first she needed the permission of the girl's stunningly sexy uncle—big-shot attorney Cameron McGrath. Cameron always had a weakness for wildly attractive women, but neither was prepared for the aftershocks of this seismic shift....

#1649 BEYOND BUSINESS—Rochelle Alers
The Blackstones of Virginia
Blackstone Farms owner Sheldon Blackstone couldn't help but be enraptured by his newly hired assistant, Renee Williams. Little did he know she was pregnant with her ex's baby. Renee was totally taken by this older man, but could she convince him to make her—and her child—his forever?

#1650 SLEEPING ARRANGEMENTS—Amy Jo Cousins
The terms of the will were clear: in order to gain her inheritance Addy Tyler needed to be married. Enter the one man she never dreamed would become her groom of convenience—Spencer Reed. Their marriage was supposed to be hands-off, but their sleeping arrangements changed everything!

SDCNM0305